# VENGEANCE ROAD

## G. MICHAEL HOPF

# DEDICATION

FOR THOSE WHO KNOW LOSS
BUT WAKE EACH DAY WITH A RENEWED
PURPOSE TO LIVE

*"If you prick us do we not bleed? If you tickle us do we not laugh? If you poison us do we not die? And if you wrong us shall we not revenge?"*

*- William Shakespeare*

# PROLOGUE

"It is only those who have neither fired a shot nor heard the shrieks and groans of the wounded who cry aloud for blood, more vengeance, more desolation. War is hell."

— William Tecumseh Sherman

## APPOMATTOX COURT HOUSE, VIRGINIA

### APRIL 9, 1865

John Nichols found it hard to look at the remaining men of the Sixty-First Georgia Infantry Regiment. Of those who stood there, only a few had been with him since its inception in 1862. Nevertheless, no matter when they joined, they all had fought hard. A good many still believed they could win and desired to fight on, but the end to the long and bitter war had finally arrived.

No one needed to ask what was going through their minds, their long gaunt faces told of hardship, sorrow and now defeat. Soon, Nichols would have to formerly surrender, a responsibility he dreaded but fell on him, as he was the most senior soldier left standing.

Several Union soldiers rode up on horses. One, a colonel by the rank insignia, dismounted and approached the haggard group. "Who's in charge?"

All eyes turned to Nichols. "Here," Nichols replied, raising his hand.

The colonel raised his brow, smoothed his thick mustache and asked, "No officers?"

"No."

"No, *sir*, is the proper reply," the colonel admonished.

"No, sir," Nichols said, forcing the words from his mouth.

"Roster?" the colonel asked.

Nichols handed him a rolled-up paper.

The colonel snatched it from his hand and unrolled it. His eyes quickly gazed over the text, and when he finished, a chuckled erupted. "This says eighty-one enlisted but only forty-nine arms."

"Yes...*sir*, that's correct," Nichols answered.

"Good thing you surrendered, not much of an army without weapons," the colonel mused.

Nichols clenched his jaw.

"Well, Corporal, form your men up and march them over to the quartermaster's, which is that way," the colonel said, pointing west. "You'll leave your arms there, and they'll give you enough rations to get home."

"That's it?" Nichols asked.

"Yes, Corporal, that's it. General Grant was gracious to you boys. If it were up to me, I'd have shot you all for treason."

Several men of the Sixty-First grumbled their disdain.

The colonel looked over Nichols' shoulder, seethed and said, "I'd keep your mouths shut, you hear?" He looked back at Nichols and continued, "Where's home?"

Shocked by the question, Nichols answered, "Georgia. Crawfordville, Georgia."

"Is that anywhere near Atlanta, or what's left of it?"

"Yes, sir."

"I heard General Sherman laid waste to it," the colonel

said with a crooked grin.

"I heard rumors, but that's about it. I haven't received a post from my wife in over six months."

"I'm not sure what you'll find, but know this, maybe you'll think twice about rebelling again. Now, take your men over to the quartermaster's."

Nichols stood without saying a word.

"You okay, Corporal?"

"Um, no, sir, I'm not."

Seeing the pain in Nichols' eyes, the colonel couldn't help but feel a tinge of sympathy. "You all fought hard; you're a tough bunch. Be proud of that at least."

Still, Nichols stood frozen, unable to speak as visions of his native Georgia ruined tortured his thoughts.

The colonel snapped his fingers.

Nichols looked up and said, "I was lost in thought."

"I can see that. You okay?"

"I'm just not sure I can just go back and pick up where I left off is all. I've been fighting for so long that it's become second nature. What do I do?"

"First thing you do, Corporal, is take that first step. Go home. Go back to Crawfordville; there you'll find your purpose again, that I promise you," the colonel said and swiftly turned around, mounted his horse and rode off with the other two junior officers following closely behind.

Several men approached Nichols. One put his hand on Nichols' shoulder and asked, "Are we sure we want to lay down our arms?"

Hearing the question, Nichols knew he had to address the men. He turned around and said, "We've all fought hard. We fought to defend our land and our way of life from an invader, but we came up short. Men of Georgia, our fight is over, but our cause can still burn in our hearts. It is now time to go home, back to our wives, mothers, fathers, and children. It is time to pick up the tools of our trade and begin again. I can't answer why the Lord God thought it best for us to lose this war, but this was his will, and we must accept it. It has been an honor to fight alongside you, but now our greatest battle is in front of us, and that is to rebuild."

Many of the men howled and cheered.

"Men of the Sixty-First Georgia, form up. The time has come to take our last steps together."

They did as he said and made three even lines.

A voice from the back row called out, "What now?"

"From here we're going to drop off our arms."

Another voice hollered, "Then what?"

"We go home."

## FIFTEEN MILES NORTHEAST OF CRAWFORDVILLE, GEORGIA

*"I intend to make Georgia howl."* – William Tecumseh Sherman

### APRIL 24, 1865

John crested the hill and stepped from the tree line. His feet were sore and his body weary. The long walk home had taken longer than he'd estimated, but soon he'd be home and in his beloved Elizabeth's arms. It had been too long since he'd seen her and his beautiful daughter, Mary; but a few more miles and he'd be crossing the threshold of his home.

He paused to take a breath and drink water. Below him the boundary of the sprawling Colonsay Plantation began; from there it covered over five hundred acres. Sitting on the far southern edge was the small nine acres he leased as a tenant farmer.

Anxious to be reunited with his family, he slung the canteen over his shoulder, picked up his sack and hurried down the hill. Along the way he marveled at the green leaves and deep blue sky; he swore the colors in Georgia were more vibrant than anywhere else and swore right then and there he'd never leave again.

He stepped out onto the first expansive field but stopped when he saw the rows of cotton that should be standing tall weren't there; instead, the field was overgrown with weeds and tall grasses. He looked around, and for as far as he could see, the fields were abandoned. Concern welled up inside him. He swiftly marched through the tall grasses towards the main house; he cleared the field and stepped onto the gravel drive. He looked left towards the ornate metal gate but saw it lying on the ground. Beyond that the large oak-lined drive led his gaze towards the manor. His eyes widened when he could see the once cloud-white exterior was streaked with black.

*Did the ravages of war reach my home too?* his mind screamed. He took off at a full sprint. Across more overgrown fields he ran until he could see the top of the chimney to his house. A small grove of lush trees now separated him from his home. He dropped his sack and pushed forward. When he exited the grove, his heart sank at the sight before him. The only thing that remained of his quaint house was the red brick chimney and the charred remains of its walls and roof. "No!" he bellowed and continued on until he reached what had been the front door. All around the home debris lay strewn, to his left the old steamer trunk Elizabeth had been given, and to his right, Mary's yellow-haired doll. He walked over and picked it up. Tears welled in his eyes as he feared the worst. Unsure what to do, he cried out, "Elizabeth, Mary!"

No reply.

"Elizabeth, it's me, John. Mary, it's your daddy. Where are you?" he yelled as he walked around the remains of the house, looking for any evidence that would be beneficial. His gaze darted to every item on the ground, from shattered lanterns, stools, the large cast-iron cauldron Elizabeth cooked his favorite stew in—all lay scattered around the barren and dead ground. Then he saw them; his eyes fixed on two small crosses in the back, under a large oak tree.

"Oh no, God, no, please say it's not, please, God, no," he cried out. He ran over to the spot and fell to his knees. Carved into the cross on the left was Elizabeth Nichols, and on the right, Mary Nichols.

Tears flowed freely down his warm cheeks, and what strength he had melted away. He collapsed to the ground and wailed. They were gone, killed, no doubt, but by whom? He dug his fingers in the loose dirt and clenched a fist. With rage in his heart, he screamed out in anger. "I promise, I swear to you both that I'll find who did this to you. I will bring justice in your name. I declare this now. I won't rest until those who perpetrated this heinous crime are dealt with."

"Mr. Nichols?" a voice boomed from behind John, startling him.

John turned to see George, the head house slave from the estate. "George, what happened?" he asked as he wiped the tears from his cheeks, leaving behind a thick smear of dirt.

"Soldiers, bummers, they did this. They done went and killed all the white folk, both here and at the manor."

"What soldiers?" John asked, standing up.

"Yankee soldiers, sir, they first came and said the slaves was free and that we could go. They then told old man Master Duke that he had to give up their guns," George said, shaking his head vigorously. "And you know Master Duke, he don't take kindly to be told what to do, especially from a Yankee soldier."

"My wife, my daughter—what happened?" John asked, stepping up to George, tears still clinging to his chin.

"I wasn't here to see, but a field slave said he saw a few of them soldiers come here. They took your wife..." George replied but paused.

"Tell me!" John insisted.

"He says they carried her outside and, well, I don't know how to say it," George said, hesitating to offer the grisly truth.

"Spit it out!" John barked.

"Sorry, sir, but I don't think you need to be hearing this," George said.

John stepped up to George and placed his hand on his shoulder. He squeezed and said, "Tell me."

Unable to look John in the eyes, George looked down and away. "They took Miss Elizabeth outside here and had their way with her. Well, sir, you knows Miss Elizabeth, she fought back; she wasn't about to let them do that without feeling her wrath. So she fought back, hit one of them soldiers real good in the head with a rock. Sir, please, I don't want to go on," George said.

"Finish."

"Well, sir, the soldiers didn't take kindly to her fighting back, so one of them came up and hit her in the head with the butt of their rifle, not once but several times."

Still gripping George's shoulder, John squeezed tighter. "And Mary?"

"I suppose Miss Elizabeth had Miss Mary hide somewhere in the house. Because shortly after they killed Miss Elizabeth, they set the house on fire. We found her body in the remains of the house. Sir, I'm so sorry," George said.

Tears again began to flow. John spun around and looked at the graves.

"Sir, is there anything I can do?" George asked.

"No."

"How about you come to the manor? I'll fix you up something to eat," George said.

"Is the entire Duke family dead?"

"Yes, sir."

"Everyone? Including little Marshal," John asked, referring to the Dukes' young son, who was five years old.

"Everyone, sir, when I say they were ruthless, they were God-awful ruthless. They killed everyone. Like I said before, they first came and told us we was free and took their guns. They gave Master Duke a real beating. A couple of hours later another group came through and did this."

"Any names? Did they at all mention who they were? What outfit they were with?" John asked.

George thought hard. "I remember one name, sir. It was the officer. He was an average fella, black hair."

"Name? Did you hear a name or unit?"

George pressed his eyes closed and dug through his memories.

"Think."

"Got it. The officer's name was Captain Pruitt, sir. Yep, that's it, Captain Pruitt, and I think one of the soldiers said something about New York."

"Cavalry or infantry?"

"I don't understand," George said.

"Were they all on horses?"

"No, sir, only the officer. The others came in on a wagon."

"Thank you, George," John said, handing him the doll and marching off.

George looked at the doll with a furrowed brow then towards John. "Sir, the manor is this way?"

"I'm not going to the manor," John said, not turning around.

"Where are you going, sir?" George asked.

"To go find this Captain Pruitt."

# CHAPTER ONE

"Revenge is an act of passion; vengeance of justice.
Injuries are revenged; crimes are avenged."
— Samuel Johnson

SANTE FE, NEW MEXICO TERRITORY

JULY 4, 1876

John meandered through the rowdy crowd, his eyes scanning for his target, Private West, whom he'd seen moments before. In and out, Private West cruised through the sea of people, making it hard for John to track him. By the dozens, a menagerie of townsfolk exited the saloons and brothels, all headed towards the edge of town to watch the fireworks celebration that was about to begin.

For whatever reason, Private West didn't have an interest, and for John, that was just fine, as long as he could find him.

"Get out of my way!" a voice screamed in anger just ahead of John. He looked and saw it was West. "I said get out of my way, you drunk bastard!" West barked and shoved a man.

The man, who was clearly drunk, mumbled something unintelligible and stumbled away.

West pushed his way past another group slipping out of the Bella Rose Saloon and ducked into Brown's Livery and Stable.

*Perfect*, John thought to himself as he rushed towards the open barn door of the livery. He looked around but didn't see West. He listened, but all his ears picked up was the sound of dozens of horses chewing, stomping and neighing. He reached down and slowly drew his Colt Single Action Army Model 1873 with a five-and-half-inch barrel. His thumb slowly drew the hammer back; the distinct clicks of the cylinder rotating were like the first notes of a concerto.

"You owe me money!" West boomed from the distant corner of the barn.

John looked and saw the shadows of two people dancing on the far wall. *West is one, but who is the other?* he thought.

"You listen here, Bill, I paid my fair share and that's that," a man spat back.

John crept closer to the room the squabbling men were in.

"That's bullshit and you know it. The deal was fifty-fifty," West roared.

"I took an additional cut because I did all the work," the man fired back while simultaneously inching his hand towards the Colt that lay on the table.

John's pace towards the door was slow, but he'd finally made it. He peeked inside and saw an unknown man sitting at a table with West towering over him. On the table in front of the man were playing cards, a pistol and a lantern.

"I gave you the heads-up on that run. You did the

job, but I provided the information, so it's fifty-fifty," West snapped, his right hand resting on the back strap of his Smith and Wesson American .44.

The man lowered his gaze and saw West's right hand. He was at a disadvantage, as his pistol was inches away. "Listen, Bill, we can work something out. How about you come back tomorrow?"

"No," West said, his right hand pressing harder against the back strap of his pistol.

The man could feel the situation was getting critical.

John stood and watched the standoff with fascination and dread. He wanted West dead, but not before getting what information he could out of him.

"Don't reach for your gun, James. You'll never get it in time," West warned after seeing James' eyes wander towards the Colt lying on the table.

"If you don't want any trouble, then I suggest you leave. Come back tomorrow. I don't have the money here anyway," James said.

"Don't lie. You don't keep your money in a bank, and I know you sleep upstairs. So if I were to guess, I'd say it was up there," West said, his gaze looking up towards the ceiling.

With West's focus somewhere else, if even for a few seconds, James knew this was his moment and made his move towards his Colt.

Seeing what was about to happen and needing West alive, John stepped into the room, raised his Colt, and squeezed off a single shot. The .45-caliber round struck James in the throat.

West jumped from the surprise entrance and gunfire. He turned, but John was on top of him. He swung down and struck West on top of the head with the butt of the pistol. West dropped to his knees. John swung again, this time striking him on the back of the head. This blow did the job; West toppled over and hit the floor, unconscious.

John looked up to find James clawing at the wound in his neck. His eyes bulged, and blood poured from his mouth. Not wanting to discharge another round for fear it would draw unwanted attention, John holstered his Colt, stepped behind James and finished the job by snapping his neck. When he laid James' lifeless head onto the table, he whispered, "I'm sorry I killed you, but I had no choice. I hope you'll find it in you to forgive me."

\*\*\*

John took a bucket of cold water and tossed it on West, who instantly woke and began to wiggle and holler.

"What's this? Who are you?" West screamed as he struggled to free himself.

While West was out cold, John had dragged him to a post and tied him to it using a thick rope he'd found in the stalls.

"Let me go and I promise I won't kill you," West declared.

John grinned and replied, "I don't think you're in any position to demand anything."

"Who are you?"

John knelt down. In his left hand he held up a

lantern, and in his right hand he held a Bowie knife. "I need you to answer a few questions."

"I'm not answering anything until you untie me," West barked.

John stared into West's dark brown eyes and asked, "Where's Captain Bartholomew Pruitt?"

West furrowed his brow. The blood that had streaked down from his head had dried and caked on his face. "Who?"

"Where's Captain Pruitt?"

"I don't know who you're talking about."

"There's an easy way or a painful way. Now I'll ask you one more time the easy way—"

Interrupting John, West snapped, "I don't know a Captain Pruitt."

Not hesitating a second, John shoved the Bowie knife into West's left arm. The blade went deep and only stopped when it struck bone.

"Argh! Damn it!" West howled.

"Answer the question."

"The hell with you—"

John twisted the blade hard to the left. "Where's Captain Pruitt?"

"Son of a bitch...oh my God, damn you!" West groaned in pain.

John twisted the blade to the right.

West seethed in pain. Sweat began to form on his brow and temples. He opened his eyes, which had been pressed closed, and asked, "If I tell you where he is, will you let me go?"

John twisted the knife again to the left and asked, "Where is he?"

"I heard he was heading to Tucson in the Arizona Territory," West said, his eyes pleading for John to remove the knife.

"What is he doing there?"

"I don't remember. He just mentioned that he was heading there—"

"When was the last time you saw him?" John asked, interrupting him.

"Eight years ago, maybe six, I can't remember, but I do recall he said Tucson. I ran into him passing through here."

A sneer cracked John's rugged face. "You swear that's what you know?"

"Yes, yes, now please remove the knife," West begged.

"One more question. Does Captain Pruitt have any distinguishing marks?"

"Marks?"

John turned the knife and replied, "Scars, birthmarks, moles—anything that can help me identify him?"

"Yeah, he has a bad scar on his right shoulder blade. It's a brand of some sort. Claims his older brother did it to him when he was a young boy. Captain Pruitt's father was a blacksmith," West said.

"What does this brand look like?"

"It was a letter *P*, about two inches tall, a real nasty-looking, thick scar, but you could clearly tell what it was," West answered.

Hearing what he wanted to hear, John pulled the knife from West's arm and stood. He wiped the blood on his trousers and slid the blade back into the sheath.

With John out of the way, West could see James' body lying on the table. "You killed him, why?"

"Because he was going to kill you. I couldn't have that," John confided.

Hoots and hollering sounded in the distance followed by a loud boom of fireworks.

"It appears the celebration has begun," John said, his thick Georgia drawl kicking in.

"You're a damn rebel!" West sneered.

"I'm a son of the South, and you, you're a damn murdering Yankee," John answered.

"What do you want with Captain Pruitt?" West asked, but as soon as the words left his lips, the answer came to him in his thoughts. "I had nothing to do with any of that. I was following orders is all."

"There was a small house on the edge of a plantation outside Crawfordville. A woman and a young girl lived there. Both were murdered."

"It wasn't me," West groaned.

John stepped towards West, causing him to cringe in fear. The once tough-talking West was now reduced to a cowering child. "That's not what Private Simmons told me when I ran into him outside Kansas City."

"He's a liar, a damn liar!" West barked. "Please, I was just a soldier, similar to you. I was only obeying orders. It was war."

John took a couple of steps and was now towering

over West. He looked down and replied, "A soldier doesn't have to obey unlawful orders. Murdering civilians is a violation of all things decent. Yes, it was war, but did my wife and daughter deserve their deaths? No, they didn't. It's one thing to fight on the battlefield, but to take the war to civilians, to your former countrymen like that is nothing short of evil. Men who do such things deserve no quarter. I have been tracking you and the other men in the detachment down for years, eleven years to be exact. After you, the only one left is Captain Pruitt." John pulled the Colt from his holster and cocked the hammer.

A wide-eyed West began to stammer, "No, no, don't. Please show mercy."

"Mercy? Like you showed my wife and daughter?" John said, raising his pistol.

The roar and pops of fireworks continued to reverberate off the walls of the room. The horses in the stalls neighed loudly and grew more agitated with each loud boom.

"Help, someone help me!" West cried out.

"No one can hear your cries."

"Please, show me mercy. I'll help you find Captain Pruitt, okay? Let's make a deal," West pleaded.

John leveled the pistol at West's head and placed his finger on the trigger.

West pressed his eyes closed and began to pray out loud. "Our Father, who art in heaven, hallowed be thy name…"

John applied more pressure to the trigger and said, "Pray all you want, but hell is where you're going." John pressed the trigger harder, causing the pistol to fire.

The single bullet did its job; West was dead.

John holstered the pistol and promptly exited the barn. He stood and looked to the brilliant fireworks display that lit the night sky.

In between the booms and pops, cheers and hoots echoed through the dirt streets of town. Everyone reveled and celebrated the country's one hundredth birthday, except for John; inside he was celebrating that he was one man closer to fulfilling the promise he'd given his beloved so many years before.

# CHAPTER TWO

"Every calling is great when greatly pursued."
– Oliver Wendell Holmes Jr.

## TUCSON, ARIZONA TERRITORY

## JULY 15, 1876

Katherine Wade loved the life of a pastor's daughter, but her life didn't start out that way. Call it fate or destiny, this life she was living now had come at great cost. While she and her family were heading to Tucson from Columbus, Ohio, their wagon train had fallen victim to a marauding horde of Apache Indians just thirty miles northeast of Tucson. She watched as the Apaches murdered her father and quickly turned their bloodthirsty rage towards her mother. If it hadn't been for the bravery of one man, Benedict Rawles, she'd be dead too. Like a white knight on his steed, Benedict rode in and slaughtered the Apaches single-handedly.

At first, she was unsure if Benedict was friend or foe; just because he'd killed the Apaches didn't mean he was a good man. When he approached her, she cowered in the back of the covered wagon and wouldn't respond to his pleas. Using all the patience he could muster, Benedict allowed her to come out on her own after he'd buried her parents.

When she exited the wagon, all she saw was his back, but when he turned, she saw the frock of a pastor. That one item soothed her worrisome thoughts, as her family was very religious and had often found solace in the pews of their church back in Ohio. With her apprehension set aside, she stood with Benedict and prayed over the graves of her parents.

Since that day, seven years past, she and he had become inseparable. Many times over the years she had wondered how a man of God knew the ways of war, but she could never muster the courage to ask. Although the few times she'd seen his scars, she could only guess he'd seen the ravages and horror of the Civil War.

Benedict kept quiet about his past except when he told her of his youth growing up in Pennsylvania. He told her he'd made the fateful decision to leave the east and venture to the west because God had given him a sign that his life's purpose was there and that he should open a church of his own. He did just that shortly after arriving in Tucson, and today marked the sixth anniversary of his congregation.

Katherine rushed out of her bedroom and called out, "Daddy, you better hurry or we'll be late."

"I'm downstairs already," he replied.

She raced down the stairs and embraced him firmly. "I don't know about you, but I'm excited."

He returned her warm embrace and said, "I think you're most excited about Miss Abigail's apple pie."

"That too." She giggled.

Benedict removed papers from his jacket pocket and handed them to her. "Please read and tell me if this is good."

"Oh, Daddy, I'm sure it's wonderful," she said, taking the papers. She unfolded them and began to read. A slight grin quickly turned to a broad smile. "Oh, it's superb. The congregation will love it."

Benedict lowered his head and sighed.

Noticing his changed demeanor, she asked, "What's wrong? There's no need to stress."

"It's not the celebration but the trip you're taking. I worry is all," he replied, referencing a planned trip to Prescott she was taking tomorrow first thing.

"I know you're worried, but I've been counting on this trip. I'm eighteen now, and these children need me."

"I know, and I'd be lying if I said I wasn't proud of you. You're something special," he said, touching her face with his open hand.

"These children weren't as fortunate as I was. They need help, and it's God's plan that I do this," she said. The children in question were orphans. Prescott had the largest orphanage in the Arizona Territory, and she was going there to volunteer her time. Many of the children at the orphanage were there because, like her, they'd lost their parents to Indian attacks or disease along the trip out west.

"I know we're not blood…"

She took his hand and said, "One doesn't need blood to deeply love someone. You not only saved my life all those years ago, but you took me in and raised me in a good home. You fed me, housed me and gave me all the things a child needs to grow up healthy and happy. And I'm so happy that you're now giving me this gift. Many parents would never allow their daughters to travel."

"I know. I'm beginning to think I'm a bad excuse for a parent," he said.

"Gosh no, you're amazing, and this adventure is God's doing. These children need me, and I'll be able to share some of the love you've given me."

Benedict glanced at the ticking clock on the mantel. "Oh dear, we need to go. Hurry to the carriage."

"I love you," she said.

"I love you too," he replied.

## FIFTY MILES NORTHEAST OF TUCSON, ARIZONA TERRITORY

John tied his horse, Molly, to a large saguaro cactus, removed his bedroll and saddlebag, and tossed them on the hard barren ground. His body ached from the long ride, and a good night's rest was poorly needed, but before he could get that, he had to set up his camp for the night.

After getting a small fire started, he unrolled his bedroll, sat down and leaned his weary back against a huge rock.

He always found the crack and pop of the fire soothing. Fires had that effect on him. His mind quickly raced back to when Mary was four years old and how they'd shared a tender moment in front of the fireplace. It would be the last time they'd do so, as the next day Fort Sumter was attacked by federal forces, and a week after, the governor of Georgia called for volunteers, and John did his duty by answering the call. Like many, he imagined the war would be over quickly, so thoughts of not seeing his family again were distant. But the war raged on and the rest was now history.

He dug into a pocket and removed his pocket watch. He pressed the latch and the cover popped open. Tucked inside was a tintype photo of Elizabeth and Mary, taken when Mary was one. He stared at the photograph and closed his eyes. He transported himself to the moment and wished he could go back there. He'd stay like that for hours sometimes, hoping that when he opened his eyes, he'd be there and they'd be looking at him with loving smiles, but it never came to be. He'd tell himself he was a fool to think he could go back to them, and the truth was, he was a fool, but only because he'd left his family vulnerable.

A coyote howled in the distance. He opened his eyes and noticed the sun had lowered beyond the mountains to the west, signaling the warm desert air would soon be giving way to the cool evening.

Forgiveness was a virtue he'd been taught from a young age and practiced often in dealings with family and friends. However, it was something that was lost to him now. He'd never forgive the men who had murdered his family, but the one individual he held the deepest contempt for was himself. He'd left his family for a cause that, no matter how valiant in spirit, couldn't be won, and in the process he'd not only lost the war but his family. The war hadn't just destroyed the Confederacy, it had destroyed a way of life for many in the South and set the

Southern states on an uncharted course.

Hunger pangs gnawed at his stomach. He opened a saddlebag and pulled out a piece of dried beef and hardtack. He took a huge bite of the beef and chewed slowly. The salty brine taste made his mouth salivate heavily.

A cool breeze swept in from the north.

He looked towards the west again, and this time thoughts came of what he'd find in Tucson. *Will I find Captain Pruitt?* But the biggest question then popped in his head. *What will I do after I kill Captain Pruitt?* So many years had been spent hunting down the murderers of his family. It was his purpose, but what would his purpose turn to afterwards? It was a question he'd never asked himself before. *Should I go back to Crawfordville? What about staying out west, starting new?* He grunted loudly. "Doesn't matter." His mind then softly told him to stay focused on the task, for there was no other purpose until he completed the one he was on.

# CHAPTER THREE

"No man has a good enough memory to be a successful liar."
– Abraham Lincoln

## TEN MILES NORTH OF TUCSON, ARIZONA TERRITORY

## JULY 16, 1876

Katherine should have known. She was kidding herself to think her father would allow her to travel without a chaperone. The hulk of a man sat opposite her in the coach and was so big his broad shoulders and massive arms infringed on the other passengers.

She attempted to strike up a conversation with him, but he would only respond with one- or two-word replies. The longest response was when he told her his name, "Call me Mr. Brown." With Mr. Brown impossible to chat with, she engaged the other passengers, Joseph and Millie, a young couple on their way to California.

"My uncle moved to San Francisco two years ago, and now he's living in a large house and even has a servant," Joseph said, his eyes wide with excitement at the prospect of following in his uncle's footsteps and finding riches in the Golden State.

"What's he doing in San Francisco?" Katherine asked with genuine curiosity.

"Textiles," Joseph replied.

"Look, this dress is made from fabric he imported from the orient. Isn't it beautiful?" Millie said as she smoothed out the front of her dress.

Katherine leaned over and examined the pale blue dress with lace trim. "It is exquisite."

"My uncle is expanding and needs help, so he sent for me. I'm to be the head of his warehousing," Joseph said.

The coach hit a large rock, jolting everyone inside.

Mr. Brown suffered the worst, as he struck the top of his head on the roof of the coach. He grunted, removed his wide-brimmed hat and examined it.

"Mr. Brown, how did my father come to employ you?" Katherine asked.

"Sheriff," he answered.

"You know Sheriff Daniels?" Katherine asked.

"Yes."

"I notice an accent; you're from?" she asked.

"Ireland."

"Where in Ireland?"

"Galway," he replied, keeping with his simple one-word answers.

A series of cracks sounded outside followed by the driver yelling, "Bandits, two o'clock!" He whipped the horse train and continued to holler.

Silence fell over everyone in the coach.

Mr. Brown removed a holstered pistol and looked outside.

The man riding shotgun called out, "Four men coming at us!"

"Go, go!" the driver yelled as he whipped the horses harder.

The speed of the coach increased enough to toss Katherine and the others around.

More cracks of gunfire sounded, followed by the roar of the double-barreled side-by-side shotgun firing.

"You missed them, Frank!" the driver hollered.

"You don't think I saw that, Ernest," Frank hollered back. He opened the breech of the shotgun, removed the empty shells, but just before he could reload, a single bullet struck him in the chest. He dropped the shotgun, which fell to the ground, and bent over in pain, and he too fell off the coach.

Katherine saw Frank fall and let out a scream at the sight.

"Yah, yah, go, go!" the driver hollered as he whipped the horses harder.

Mr. Brown spotted a bandit closing in. He leaned over Katherine and took a shot, but it missed. He cocked the pistol and fired again. This time his aim was true; the bullet struck the bandit's horse. The horse tumbled to the ground and tossed the rider. Mr. Brown cocked the hammer again and looked for more bandits.

"Left side!" Katherine called out, seeing two men coming towards them at an angle.

Mr. Brown pivoted as best he could inside the tight coach, took aim and fired. His shot missed. He cocked and fired again, once more missing the moving targets.

The men on the horses returned fire; both shots struck Mr. Brown, one in the shoulder and one in his side. The bullet that hit him in the side went clean through and hit Millie in the chest.

Katherine's eyes darted around the frantic and chaotic coach. It appeared her father had been wise in having Mr. Brown come, but even with him, there wasn't any guarantee she'd survive.

Mr. Brown grunted in pain from his wounds; however, those weren't enough to stop him. He raised his pistol and fired. This time the round hit one of the bandits, who slid off his horse. But no sooner had Mr. Brown found success than the bandits scored another victory when a bullet ripped through the frame of the door and struck him in the forehead. Mr. Brown's massive physique dropped to the floor like a heavy sack.

Katherine's instincts took over. She picked up Mr. Brown's pistol, cocked it, took aim and pulled the trigger. The hammer fell, but nothing happened. Unfamiliar with handguns, she looked at it oddly, cocked it again and tried one more time. Once more the hammer struck and it didn't fire. The pistol was out of ammunition. She turned to Joseph and said, "I need help."

Joseph didn't look up. His attention was on his wife, who lay in his lap.

Two shots cracked outside.

From the corner of Katherine's eye, she saw the driver of the coach fall to the ground. "I need help reloading this!" she hollered.

Joseph looked up, his face smeared with blood and tears. "Give it to me," he said, holding out his hand.

Two riders came up alongside the coach, one on

each side, took the reins of the horses and slowed the coach until they got it to stop.

Joseph fumbled trying to reload the pistol, his shaking hands turning the cylinder.

"Hurry!" Katherine pleaded.

"Put it down," one of the bandits said followed by the familiar clicks of a hammer being cocked.

Joseph looked up, saw the muzzle of a pistol and froze. He dropped the half-loaded pistol on the floor and raised his hands.

Katherine felt a strong temptation to pick it up, her eyes darting to it and the bandit pointing the pistol.

"Don't try it," the bandit said, clearing his throat. "Put your hands up."

The second bandit dismounted and ran to the door of the coach. He tossed it open, peered inside with a broad smile and said, "How do you do?"

\*\*\*

The first sounds of gunfire forced John to slow Molly to a trot and pay close attention to any subsequent shots. The second volley told him the precise direction and piqued his curiosity as to what might be happening. He nudged Molly and poked her gently with a spur.

Ever obedient, she did as he needed and began to head in the direction of the gunfire.

The fury of the fire grew the closer he came. A small rocky rise rose before him, and by the way the sound carried, he had a strong hunch the battle was on the other side.

Molly took him close to the crest but stopped when John pulled back on her reins.

He jumped off, pulled his Winchester Model 1873 from the leather scabbard, grabbed his binoculars and raced up the hill, clearing the remaining twenty feet in seconds. He got low and crawled until he could see over the other side. Below him he saw a coach with a four-horse team stopped on the road. A woman and man were kneeling behind the coach, with a single man pointing a pistol at them while another pulled luggage and trunks from the coach and tossed them onto the ground. Needing to get a better look, he put his binoculars to his face and peered through.

The woman, who was Katherine, knelt with a look of terror on her face. The male passenger, Joseph, not only displayed a look of fear but also sorrow. One of the bandits towered over them. He was talking and waving his pistol. John adjusted a bit and zoomed in on the second bandit. It was then he got a good look at the carnage inside the coach. There he saw a man, Mr. Brown, and a woman, Millie, lying dead.

An inner debate began to rage inside him. Should he intervene, or should he go about his business? Getting involved was risky on a couple of fronts. Any time spent focused on anything else but pursuing Captain Pruitt put him that much further away from completing his mission, and second, he could get himself killed.

He lowered the binoculars and thought. He weighed the pros and cons and kept coming up with more cons.

Katherine screamed.

John looked up and saw the bandit dragging her back to the coach. He knew what that meant. Visions of his wife being treated that way came front and center. He needed to act and now. He dropped the binoculars, lifted his rifle and put it into his shoulder. He raised the rear sight and adjusted it for distance. When he was ready, he settled in behind the sights, his cheek welded perfectly to the rear stock, and he placed his index finger on the trigger.

The bandit pushed Katherine up against the coach. He was ripping at her dress, but her resistance was making it hard for him.

John had a clear shot. He squeezed the trigger until it went off. His first shot was true, striking the first bandit in the back of the head. Not hesitating, he moved the lever action and loaded another .44-40 round into the chamber and began to search for the second bandit. He found him hiding on the far side of the coach.

Katherine shoved the bandit's dead body off her and raced for cover, unsure who was shooting.

A bullet ricocheted just below John, kicking up a puff of dirt. He aligned the sights on the man's partially exposed head and squeezed. The bullet roared out of the barrel but struck the side of the coach, missing the man. John worked the action once more and took aim. He looked for the man but now couldn't see him.

Katherine had stopped to untie Joseph.

The second bandit appeared from behind the coach, atop his horse.

Seeing his chance, John took aim and let another round loose. This time he struck the man between the shoulder blades. He instantly fell to the ground, face-first.

Katherine looked up towards John but was unable to see him

With the threat neutralized, John got up, mounted his horse and rode down to the coach. As he approached, he found Katherine pointing a pistol at him. He held his hands high and said, "Easy there, little lady. I'm your white knight. I mean you no harm."

"How do I know that?" she asked.

"Are you a marshal?" Joseph asked.

"No, sir, just a man passing through," John answered calmly.

"You're not going to rob us?" Joseph asked.

John lowered his hands, leaned against the horn of the saddle and quipped, "This isn't how you usually thank people for saving your life?"

"We're scared is all," Katherine said.

"Well, ma'am, I'm not here to hurt, rob, steal, or any number of bad things. I heard the gunfire and against my greater judgment decided to come help out."

"Your better judgment?" she asked.

"Yes, ma'am, now would you like me to help further?" John asked.

Katherine looked at Joseph, who nodded. She turned back to John and asked, "If your judgment allows, would you mind helping us load the coach back up?"

"That I can do," John said, dismounting. He walked over to a trunk, picked it up and placed it on the back of the coach.

Joseph went to deal with his wife's body while Katherine slid the pistol into a deep pocket of her skirt and helped pick up smaller items strewn on the ground. "Who does this?"

Hauling another heavy trunk, John replied, "Evil men, the world is full of them."

Frustrated more than shocked, Katherine blurted out, "Father will never allow me to leave again. There goes Prescott and the School for Wayward Children."

"The School for Wayward Children?" John asked.

"Long story, but it's where I was heading, as a volunteer not a resident," she clarified.

"You look young, but I wasn't confused. You look older than eighteen."

Joseph appeared and began to help.

John looked at Joseph and said with sincerity, "I'm sorry for your loss."

A tear appeared in Joseph's eye. All he could do was nod, for if he replied, he might start to wail.

"It was horrible. Any idea who they might be?" Katherine asked both men.

"I have no idea. But my experience has always shown, if there's a town, there's always road agents or bandits along its roads on the outskirts," John said.

"They're white men, must be Captain's Raiders," Joseph said.

"Captain's Raiders?" John asked, intrigued by the name.

Katherine paused and raised a brow. "I think Daddy

mentioned them before."

"Word around town is they're a group of outlaws whose leader is a former captain in the US Army. Each time a US Marshal has come in to take care of them, the marshal is always found dead. But this is odd," Joseph said.

"Odd, why?" John asked, his intrigue turning to desire for knowledge.

"'Cause Captain's Raiders haven't been seen in these parts for some time. Rumors were they had fled to Mexico," Joseph said, picking up the last piece of luggage and tossing it on top of the coach.

"His name, what's the captain's name?" John asked, taking Joseph by the arm.

Joseph gave John an odd look and replied, "I don't know his name. He just goes by the Captain."

"You don't know his full name?" John asked, his grasp growing tighter around Joseph's small arm.

"You're hurting me," Joseph complained.

"What's his full name?" John again asked with urgency.

"Listen, Mister, I don't know his name. No one does. Now please let go of my arm," Joseph said.

Realizing he was scaring Joseph and Katherine, John let go. He looked at Joseph and said, "I apologize, forgive me."

Joseph rubbed his arm and said, "It's fine. But something tells me you're looking for the Captain."

"I'm looking for a man and he was a captain in the Union Army, so if *the Captain* is that same man, then yes,

I'm looking for the Captain."

"I'd suggest you talk to the sheriff. He might be able to help you," Joseph said. He chuckled slightly and continued, "Sheriff Daniels isn't going to like hearing Captain's Raiders are back. The poor man can barely keep deputies on the payroll."

John noted the last comment but didn't reply.

"And my father, he might be able to help too. He knows many people in the community. He's a pastor," Katherine said.

John only nodded.

Katherine wasn't sure what to make of John or that small incident, but her intuition, which she trusted more than not, told her John was a good, but troubled, man.

"Will you be coming back to town with us?" Katherine asked.

"Is that town Tucson?" John asked.

"Yes, it is," she answered.

"Then, yes, I'll escort you both back to town," John replied.

## TUCSON, ARIZONA TERRITORY

Once Joseph and the bodies of Millie, Mr. Brown, Frank and Ernest were deposited with the undertaker, John headed towards Katherine's house.

"Last house on the right," she hollered from the coach.

He pulled the coach up near the front porch stairs and brought the horses to a halt. He engaged the wheel brake and hopped off.

The front door of the house burst open. "Katherine, what in heaven are you doing here?" Benedict said loudly, rushing towards her.

The two embraced.

"Oh, Daddy, it was horrible, just horrible," she cried.

He broke his embrace to get a good look at her. "Were you hurt?"

"Just shaken, but I was the lucky one. They killed the poor woman who was riding with us, as well as the drivers; and Mr. Brown is dead too," she confessed.

"Oh my," he said, pulling her back close. "It's by God's grace you survived, then."

She looked back at John and said, "If it was God's grace, then God sent this man to help us."

Benedict let go of Katherine and walked up to John, who was unloading the coach for Katherine. Benedict extended his hand and said, "I have you to thank for saving my daughter and returning her to me."

John looked at Benedict, gave him a slight grin, took his hand and firmly shook it. "You're welcome."

"It was awful, Daddy. Four men attacked us. Mr. Brown stopped two of them and..." she said before pausing once she realized she didn't know John's name. "I'm so sorry, in all the drama I didn't get your name. I apologize."

"It's John," he answered, still shaking Benedict's hand.

"Just John?" Benedict asked.

"John...Smith," John lied.

"Do I hear a Southern drawl?" Benedict asked.

"Yes, sir, I'm from Alabama," John again lied. The last thing he wanted was his real name floating around town.

Benedict cut his eyes slightly and said, "Hmm."

"You ever been to Alabama?" John asked then added, "Sorry, I didn't get your name."

"I'm Benedict Rawles, and this is my daughter, Katherine," Benedict said. "And no, I've never been to Alabama before. I hear it's a beautiful place, at least before the war."

"Pleased to meet you, but I only wish it were under better circumstances," John said. "I'm just about finished, and after that I'll leave you two. I just need to know where the Overland stagecoach office is."

"I'll get you directions; it's quite easy," Benedict said, stepping away from John.

"Do you have a place to stay?" Katherine asked.

"Not yet, if you have the name of a good and reputable hotel, I'd be grateful," John said.

Katherine stepped forward and took Benedict's arm. "Oh, Daddy, we can't have him staying in an old dusty hotel. We have the spare room; he can stay here." She looked at John and continued, "I'm sure Mr. Smith would be grateful for a hot meal served on a family table."

Benedict looked reluctant, as did John, at the suggestion.

"I'm sure Mr. Smith would prefer his privacy," Benedict said.

"I appreciate the offer, but I wouldn't want to

intrude," John said.

"Nonsense, you came to my aid, and now we will come to yours. Stay one night or ten, doesn't matter. I owe you my life, and Daddy says one must always pay their debts," Katherine said, approaching John and placing her small hand on his shoulder.

The gentle touch of a young, beautiful woman sent a warm shiver through John's body. He looked deep into her blue eyes and relented. "If you insist, but first let me take the coach back to the Overland."

"Wonderful," Katherine said. She turned and saw a look of consternation on Benedict's face. She walked up to Benedict, leaned in and whispered, "Don't be rude, Daddy."

"Ahh, yes, this is wonderful," Benedict said, grinding his teeth.

John could tell his overnight stay at their house was the last thing Benedict wanted, but he had always been a sucker for a woman's approach, and secondly, he had a lot of questions for Benedict concerning the Captain. "I'll be off now. See you both near sundown." He jumped onto the coach, but before he departed, he glanced in Katherine's direction and saw she was looking at him too. He tipped his hat and headed off.

\*\*\*

John tied Molly to the hitching post outside the sheriff's office. He straightened out his weathered clothes as best he could and patted off any excess dust that had accumulated in the fabric. He adjusted his gun belt and holster and headed up the wooden steps.

The door to the office opened, and out stepped two men wearing badges. They were tall, lean and both sported thick mustaches. They gave John a skeptical look and walked off.

John walked through the open door and entered the sheriff's office. To his left a large oak desk sat covered in papers. In the far corner was an oil lamp and next to it a set of keys, no doubt to the cells in the back. A burly man sat behind the desk, his feet upon it and his hands resting on a pooch of a belly. He was an older man, and if John had to guess, he'd say he was in his fifties. Like the younger men he'd seen exiting, he also sported a thick and bushy mustache that curled down below his lower lip. Behind the desk, a gun rack sat with half a dozen Winchester rifles. The office was smaller than he'd imagined for a city of Tucson's size. "Excuse me, I'm looking for the sheriff," John said.

"You found him. How can I be of service?" the sheriff replied.

"My name is John Smith. I had an encounter with a couple of men from Captain's Raiders this morning along the northern road."

"You did, did ya?" the sheriff asked. "We just got wind of that. I sent a couple of deputies to investigate. How about you pull up a chair and tell me what happened?" Daniels said, taking his feet off the desk and grabbing a piece of paper.

John did as he said and sat down on one of two

small wooden chairs in front of the desk. He removed his hat and placed it in his lap.

"Were you a traveler on the Overland coach to Phoenix?" Daniels asked.

"No, sir, I happened to hear gunfire and came upon two men robbing the coach," John answered.

The sheriff looked up and asked, "Where are you from? I note a hint of the South in your voice."

"I'm originally from Alabama, sir," John replied.

"And what brings a man from all the way back in Alabama to Tucson? Are you looking to escape the humidity for the dry heat?" Daniels joked.

Recalling Joseph's last comment while on the road, John quickly answered, "In search of work as a lawman, sir."

The sheriff looked up and furrowed his bushy brow. "How do you know I'm looking for deputies?"

"Well, sir, word spreads fast, and I'm here to offer my service if you'll take it. I'm a hard worker, good with a gun, and most importantly know how to follow orders," John said, hoping his brief list of qualifications would suffice.

"Were you in the army?" Daniels asked.

John hesitated to reply, not knowing the sheriff's bias against the Confederacy. "Um, yes, sir."

"I'm assuming the South?"

"Yes, sir."

"I was here when you rebels occupied Tucson. I'd have to admit that life wasn't so bad. Listen, I'm not sure I can bring a Confederate on. I'm already dealing with issues now, and to have someone like you would only add controversy."

"I can understand, but maybe I can help unofficially," John offered.

"How's that?"

"This group of marauders, the Captain's Raiders, what can you tell me about them?"

"They've been a thorn in this town's side for a few years now. We haven't heard from them for some time, many began to wonder if they'd moved on permanently, but it appears that may not be true. The thing is those men who attacked the stagecoach today may not be connected to the Captain. They could just be random outlaws."

John thought that nothing about today's attack was unique or offered anything of a clue about who they were or where they came from.

"The two deputies you saw leave were heading to the Overland Stage Company to interview them. How you can help is go there and meet up with them, take them to the site. I want to bring those men's bodies back for proper identification. Can you do that?"

"Sure."

"Who knows, if you show my deputies you're a good man, maybe I'll find a place for you. God knows I need the help."

"I have a question."

"Shoot," the sheriff said, pulling out a pipe from the desk drawer and packing it with a rich-smelling tobacco.

"The Captain, who is he? What's his real name?"

John asked.

Daniels struck a match and hovered it over the chamber of the pipe and puffed several times. The tobacco fired up and burned; a whiff of smoke made its way to John. The smell was sweet and reminded John of his former commanding officer back with the Sixty-First Georgia. "We've been trying to hunt him down for years, but all we know is he's a former army captain from back east, nothing more than that."

"Not a name, nothing?" John pressed.

"No, some say he's a war veteran who came out west to start new but fell on tough times, so he turned to robbing stagecoaches and pilfering farms. He's a mean old bastard. Has a deep thick scar across his face and a thick Northern accent."

"Like a New York accent?"

"You have many questions, don't you?"

"Just curious is all. I can't tell you how much I'd appreciate getting to work for you. I came all this way with hopes that I'd find gainful employment as a deputy. How about I help your deputies, and if I do a good enough job, you'll reconsider?"

The sheriff took several puffs and exhaled a thick plume of smoke. "I can do that. Now go find my deputies; tell them Sheriff Daniels sent you."

John stood and said, "Yes, sir." He turned and headed towards the door.

"Hey, Johnny Reb," Daniels called out.

John hated that moniker but was willing to suffer it in order to win Daniels' favor. "Yes, Sheriff," John said, stopping and facing the sheriff.

"Let's keep your past between us. I didn't mind the Confederate occupation years back, but some didn't take to it kindly and have bad memories of that period."

"My lips are sealed, sir."

"And tone down that drawl of yours, it's like you're wearing a sign that reads *Johnny Reb*."

"I'll do my best, sir."

"Do your best and then some."

John thought and replied with a less twangy sound, "Yes, sir."

"Good man. Now hurry before you miss them," Daniels said, waving him away.

John exited the office and paused out front. He wasn't an overtly proud man, nor would he ever go straight to fisticuffs to defend Dixie, but having to change how he spoke did annoy him. He practiced saying a few things in his new dialect and found it not too hard. If pretending to be someone entirely different and lying led him to Captain Pruitt, then so be it. The ends would justify the means.

\*\*\*

Benedict paced the front living room of the house, mumbling to himself.

Katherine watched from the wingback chair. She was familiar with this type of behavior and knew that it usually led to Benedict going through a range of emotions. It started with anger then quickly would morph into isolation. He was never violent, nor would he emotionally torture her, he would simply vent but do so with a tone not fitting of a pastor. It was a side of him that only she knew.

"I knew something would happen. I just knew it! I'm a fool!" he barked out loud.

She was tempted to respond but sat pensively waiting for his tirade to end.

"How could I be so foolish? You're safe, and I thank God for that, but now we have a strange man, a Confederate, in our midst. No doubt he was, I can hear it in his voice," he blared to himself. He clasped his hands together and said, "Lord God, give me patience and temperance. I know you do this to test me."

Unable to withhold commenting, she opened up. "Daddy, had I known you held a prejudice against people from the South, I wouldn't have invited him to stay. I only felt an obligation to assist the man who saved my life. I did as you always taught me. I looked upon him simply as a man, one of God's creations, with no judgment based upon where he may have come from but through his actions."

Benedict paused his pacing and looked at her. "My dear Katherine, there are many things you don't know about me, meaning my past. I don't talk about it much. I fight these demons every day."

She sprang up and took his hands in hers. "Oh, Father, what torments you?"

"Before I came out west, I served in the Union Army. I met many a Confederate on the battlefield and found them to be ruthless killers who defended the atrocity of slavery with their dying breath. Now one of those men are here and will be under my roof."

"Daddy, you don't know his past. You only just met him."

"I can see it in his eyes. He's a killer."

Katherine thought hard about Benedict's last comment. It was true that John was a killer, she'd witnessed it with her own eyes, but his acts weren't for pleasure or to fulfill a sick agenda. No, he killed so that others might live. His killing was righteous. "I can't pretend to know what haunts you from that dreadful war, but please give this man the benefit of the doubt. And just because he killed those men, he did so to save my life. Don't you remember when you did the very same thing for me all those years ago?"

He sighed and said, "Am I a good father?"

"You aren't my birth father, but in the years we've spent together, you have been a better father than I could have ever had God bless me with."

"My dear, do you trust this man?"

"I do."

"Then I will defer to your better judgment 'cause mine is lacking after having allowed the most precious gift to almost slip through my hands. I just pray you'll forgive me."

"Oh, Daddy, there's nothing to forgive. I'm a woman now and I made that decision to leave. I'm just saddened that I had to witness once more how evil men can be, but I'll add this. What happened today has hardened me to work even harder for God and to spread his word."

He embraced her and said, "What did I do to deserve you?"

She returned his embrace and quickly pulled away. "Now, let me go prepare the room for our guest."

"Go," he said with smiling eyes.

She raced upstairs.

He watched her scale the stairs until she was out of sight. With her gone, his composure changed, his jaw tightened, and his glare turned sour. It would take every ounce of willpower he had not to prejudge John and hold him accountable for the crimes he'd encountered during the war.

\*\*\*

John's excursion back to the site of the attack proved beneficial. He provided much-needed information to the deputies, and they in turn answered many of his questions, except one. What was the Captain's name? It appeared no one knew who he was or exactly where he'd come from; he was an enigma. One surprise development of the ride was coming upon the sole survivor of the robbery. The bandit who'd had his horse shot out from underneath him was alive but badly injured. They brought him back and locked him in a cell to await a doctor's visit. When he could talk, Daniels planned on interrogating him.

Weary from the long day, John longed to rest in an actual bed. He tied Molly outside and walked up to the front door of Benedict's house. He raised his hand to knock, but the door flew open before he could.

"You must be utterly famished. Please come in," Katherine said.

John looked at her and smiled. "I am, but first I'd like to get my horse in the barn and fed. She worked harder than I did today."

"How about I help with that?" Benedict said, showing up from out of nowhere. He stepped past Katherine and out onto the porch alongside John.

"No, I got it. Just show me where," John said.

"I'd prefer we go together," Benedict insisted.

Katherine cut her eyes slightly at Benedict, but she couldn't refuse her father. She nodded and said, "When you both are done, wash up. I'll have dinner on the table."

John tipped his hat and followed Benedict, who was already headed towards the barn with Molly in tow. He caught up and said, "I want to thank you—"

Benedict cut him off, stopped walking and stared at John. "I might be a simple pastor, but don't mistake the fact that I'm a Godly man for a pacifist. That woman in there, my daughter, she's everything to me, and if you think, if you have some design on—"

"Whoa, whoa, whoa, I didn't invite myself. If you want me to go, just say the word."

"You can stay, but don't get any ideas," Benedict warned.

"I don't have any ideas except a hot home-cooked meal and a nice warm bed," John said.

"And that's all you'll get. If you even give her a favorable look, I'll gut you," Benedict snarled.

"Understood," John said, a slight grin appearing on his face. He was impressed with Benedict; he was definitely not the typical pastor type.

Benedict only stared now, the orange glow of the sunset casting a warm shine upon his face. John noticed the numerous scars and wondered how he'd gotten them. From his demeanor, talk and physicality, Benedict had had a harder past than that of an altar boy. It intrigued him. The question then popped in his head, who was Benedict?

\*\*\*

The savory smell of biscuits was the first thing that hit John's nostrils. His mouth began to water, and he prayed they had butter because the thought of rich salty butter on a hot biscuit sounded about perfect right then.

He entered the dining room to find Benedict sitting at the head of the table and two additional places set, next to Benedict but across from each other. He stood and waited to be invited to take one.

"Have a seat," Benedict said somberly.

John moved towards the table when Katherine appeared from the kitchen with a cast-iron skillet in her hands. "You're here, good. Take that seat," she said, nodding towards the one closest to the window. He did as she said and settled in. He stared at the place setting. It seemed foreign to him after so many years without having a proper dinner.

Katherine put the skillet on the table and took the seat across from him.

Benedict looked at her, smiled and said, "Let us pray." He took Katherine's hand and lowered his head; she followed suit.

John tipped his head down but kept peeking up as Benedict recited a common dinner prayer. When he was finished, he paused and continued with his own words, "Heavenly Father, I have something else to especially be thankful for today. Your holy light shielded my beautiful daughter and kept her safe. Thank you, Lord. Amen."

"Amen and thank you, Lord, for my savior, John Smith," Katherine said.

John lifted his head, smiled and nodded.

Benedict couldn't hide his aggravation. As Katherine went to serve the flank steak, he leered at John.

"I hope you like the meat. Daddy got it special today from the butcher," she said, placing a four-ounce piece on his plate. "Potatoes?"

John nodded.

"String beans? They're from my own garden," she said, scooping up a spoonful and putting them next to the roasted potatoes.

John's eyes scanned the table until he spotted the covered basket.

Katherine grabbed it and asked, "Biscuit?"

"Yes, ma'am," he said happily.

She placed a biscuit on his plate then proceeded to serve Benedict.

John saw a bowl of butter and, using his knife, took a glob and placed it in the flaking center of the biscuit so it would melt through. He leaned back and looked at his plate. He hadn't seen so much great food on his plate, much less a plate, in many years. A feeling of gratefulness swept over him. He looked at Katherine and said, "Thank you." He gave Benedict a look and again said, "Thank you, sir. Your hospitality is appreciated."

"Of course, this is how we treat our heroes," she said.

Benedict nodded and went back to cutting his steak.

"John, tell us about Alabama. Where are you from there?" Katherine asked.

Thinking quickly, he blurted out the first town that came to mind, "Birmingham, ma'am."

"Oh, is it nice? I've never been," she asked.

"It's fine, I suppose."

"Daddy is from Harrisburg, Pennsylvania; born and raised. I'm from Ohio, a small nothing town called Marion," she said as she took a stab at a wedge of potato.

Confused by how she'd phrased her comment, John asked, "How is it you're from Pennsylvania and you're from Ohio?"

Benedict sighed heavily, signaling his displeasure with the topic.

Not wanting to upset him, Katherine said, "It's where I was born and where he was born; that's what I meant, nothing more."

John knew she was lying. How? Because he was a master at telling tall tales.

"Katherine tells me you're looking for someone, and that someone might be the Captain himself," Benedict said.

John gave Katherine a look then turned his attention to Benedict. "I'm looking for a man who was a captain in the Union Army during the war."

"And you think the Captain could be this man?" Benedict asked.

"Maybe. Do you know who the Captain is? Do you know his name?" John asked. "I've been asking anyone who might know, and not a soul does. I spoke with Sheriff Daniels, his deputies, and the men at the Overland. Everyone knows the Captain, but not who he is or where he came from."

Katherine reached over and touched Benedict's hand. "One of the reasons I wanted John to meet you is I told him you know many people, being a pastor."

"I do know a lot of people; it's a blessing of my job. Tell me, John, this captain you're looking for, how do you know him?"

John was tempted to tell the truth but thought it best to keep it to himself for fear Captain Pruitt was an unlikely friend of theirs. "We're old friends, believe it or not. I heard he came out here, and I wanted to meet up with him. If my old friend turned to robbery, I'd be greatly disappointed."

"Old friends, hmm, when did you meet?" Benedict asked.

"After the war," John answered, which was partially true; he'd come to know who Pruitt was after the war.

Benedict cut a piece of steak and shoved it into his mouth. "I don't know any former captains from the army. You know, what might help me is this man's name."

"Captain Bartholomew Pruitt," John replied.

Benedict coughed loudly.

"Daddy, are you okay?" Katherine asked, noticing Benedict was having a difficult time breathing.

He coughed more aggressively and pounded on his chest a few times. "Sorry, went down the wrong pipe."

John gave him a curious look and asked, "Have you heard of this man before?"

"No, never, but that's not to say he doesn't live in Tucson or that he's the infamous Captain of the Raiders," Benedict replied. Sweat beaded on his forehead. He coughed again, wiped his mouth with a napkin and said, "If you'll excuse me, I'm going to walk a bit."

"Daddy?" Katherine asked, concerned.

"I'm fine, just inhaled that big piece of food. You and our guest finish your dinner. And, Katherine, keep the conversation polite," Benedict said and walked out.

John raised a brow. Something told him that Pruitt's name had triggered that response, and if it had, he would need to find out.

# CHAPTER FOUR

"Always mystify, mislead and surprise the enemy if
possible."
– Stonewall Jackson

## TUCSON, ARIZONA TERRITORY

## JULY 17, 1876

John woke early and immediately headed to the sheriff's
office. He wanted to know if the prisoner had spoken or
revealed anything. He decided to walk instead of ride to
give Molly a much-needed break. She was a good horse
and treated him well, so when he could, he returned the
favor. As he walked the dusty and relatively busy streets
of Tucson, he looked at every man that walked by him
and questioned if that was Pruitt. He had never met the
man, and all he had to identify him were descriptions
given by the men in his detachment. The unfortunate
thing was Pruitt's description could fit many men: he was
average height, dark hair, brown eyes, and his facial
features were normal. The one distinguishing mark could
only be seen with his shirt off, not an easy task.
Something told him that though he was close, finding
Pruitt would prove to be the most difficult of any he'd
tracked down.

He cleared the corner of First Street to find Daniels
standing out front of his office, arguing with a well-
dressed man in his forties. He couldn't hear what they

were talking about, but by the animated hand gestures and body language, the conversation was heated. Not one who was afraid of most things, John proceeded up to the two men.

John tipped his hat and said, "Good morning, Sheriff Daniels."

"What the hell do you want?" the man growled at John.

"I'm here to see the sheriff," John replied.

"We're having a private conversation. Now go find somewhere else to loiter," the man replied.

John grinned at the man.

Daniels gave John a look and replied, "Best you go." He turned his attention back to the man and continued where he'd left off. "I'm not going to dignify your accusations. Now I suggest you leave before I arrest you for harassment."

"How dare you talk to me like that," the man said, jabbing his index finger into Daniels' chest.

Daniels shook his head and said, "You don't listen, do you?"

"I don't think he does," John quipped.

The man looked at John and in a fit of anger gave John a shove. "I said to back off."

Not one to be pushed around or intimidated, John came at the man. He grabbed a fistful of cravat and shirt and sneered, "Push me again and you'll wish you heeded the sheriff's suggestion to leave a minute ago."

The man cut his eyes at John and said, "Get your hands off me."

"John, unhand Mr. Geist," Daniels ordered.

John did as Daniels said.

The man grumbled under his breath as he smoothed out his neckwear and shirt. He glared at Daniels then gave the same look to John before turning around and marching off.

"It appears he's a bit upset with you," John joked.

"It's my life, but next time I say it's best you go, *go*," Daniels snorted.

"I apologize," John said.

"What can I do you for?"

"I thought I'd come back and check in, see if you'd reconsidered my offer to work," John said.

"Sorry, but I've had a lot going on, and with all the trouble Mr. Geist is causing me, I don't need another scandal by hiring a Confederate."

"The war ended over a decade ago," John countered.

"Son, that war stirred up some hard feelings that I feel won't ever go away. Now, I appreciate the help yesterday. If you're in need of work, I can put a good word out for you with some of the inns and brothels. I know they're always looking for security."

"I'm not interested in being someone's hired gun. I was hoping to be given a chance to be a lawman," John said.

The door to the sheriff's office opened, and a deputy by the name of Garrett stuck his head out. "Sheriff, he's talking."

Daniels headed inside without saying another word to John.

John followed right behind him, nodding to Garrett, whom he'd met yesterday. "Morning, Garrett."

"Mornin', John," Garrett said, returning the nod. He caught up to Daniels and said, "When I mean he's talking, I don't mean he's giving usual information."

"Understood," Daniels said.

"And, Sheriff, he says his name is Watch Eye Ferguson."

Daniels raised his brow and shook his head. "What is it with these outlaws and their idiotic names?" Ready to begin his interrogation, Daniels walked up to the cell and stopped a few feet from the bars. "I hear you have something to say."

Ferguson slowly sat up. He clearly was favoring his left side. The fall from the horse had resulted in a broken shoulder and multiple lacerations along that side of his body. "Yeah, I have something to say."

"Spit it out," Daniels said.

Ferguson grinned, showing his blackened teeth. "I suggest you open that cell door and let me go."

A look of shock appeared on Daniels' face. He cocked his head and said, "Funny that a man sitting in my jail cell is talking as if he's at an advantage. Let me give you some advice, open up about who you are and what group you're running with, and I'll make sure the noose is loose."

Ferguson stood up and limped forward until he reached the door of the cell. He grasped a bar, leaned in and sneered, "Let me give you some advice, Sheriff. If you don't want the Captain to come in here and kill you all, you'll open this door, give me my irons and let me go."

Daniels recoiled from the brash behavior. An uneasy chuckle left his mouth before he said, "So you're with Captain's Raiders? That's one of my questions. Now, where is your hideout?"

Ferguson spit in Daniels' face.

The usual calm demeanor melted away from Daniels. He pulled out his keys and unlocked the cell door. "Come here, you son of a bitch!" Daniels barked as he entered the cell, his fists raised.

Ready to fight, Ferguson threw a punch, but it was easily avoided by Daniels, who countered with a closed fist across Ferguson's jaw. The punch was decisive, causing Ferguson to stumble and fall back onto the cot.

Daniels pursued and leveled one punch after another on Ferguson, who responded by laughing like a madman.

Confused by the response to the beating, Daniels stopped his assault and looked down at the battered and bleeding man. "You're crazy, you know that?"

"Come on, Sheriff! Is that all you got, old man!" Ferguson howled with laughter.

Daniels stepped back and slowly exited the cell, locking it when he was outside.

"You're all going to die, you hear me, you're all going to die!" Ferguson screeched.

Garrett leaned in to Daniels and asked, "Want me to shut him up?"

"No, I think he actually enjoys the pain. Just leave him to scream. I do need you to go see the magistrate. I want to have this son of a bitch swinging by nightfall," Daniels said and exited the office.

John followed Daniels outside and said, "Let him go."

"What?"

"Give him what he wants. Let him go," John again insisted.

"Are you sick in the head? Why on God's green earth would I do that?" Daniels asked.

"Because he'll lead us right to the Captain's hideout, that's why. I'll follow him right back to the rat's nest."

"I can't risk that. Plus he'll know if we let him go that we're up to something," Daniels said.

"Fake it. Make him think he escaped. Leave the cell open, something like that. Leave the keys where he can get them. And when he escapes, I'll follow him back to the hole he came from," John said, a look of excitement on his face.

"It's a huge risk, and if I were to do such a thing, who says you'd be the one following him. I don't even know you," Daniels said, his arms crossed firmly across his chest.

"Deniability. Hire me; let me be the fall guy. Don't you see it?" John pressed.

Daniels smoothed his mustache with his thick fingers and grunted. His mind ran through all the scenarios that could go right or go horribly wrong.

"Well?" John asked.

It was a monumental risk for Daniels, but he was willing to take it. With Geist breathing down his neck and causing all sorts of trouble in town, he needed a win, but not a normal win. He needed a big win. If he could finally take out the Captain, he'd be hailed as a hero. It wasn't John's rationale of having him as a fall guy that was so convincing, it was the possibility to cement his legacy as a lawman. He turned to John and said, "I like it! Johnny Reb, you're hereby appointed deputy. Now let's go plan this out."

\*\*\*

Benedict woke to the smell of bacon. As he got dressed, he played through the conversation he'd have to handle John. It was his intention to inform him that he needed to leave. When he exited his bedroom, he heard Katherine singing in the kitchen. Just yesterday she'd been assaulted, and today she was singing. He entered the kitchen and said, "Good morning, sweetheart." He went up to her and gave her a peck on the forehead.

"Good morning, Daddy," she said with a smile.

"You're very happy today," he said, taking a seat at the small table in the kitchen.

"'Cause it's a beautiful day and the blue sky is calling me to go outside," she said, looking out the window at the blue sky.

"The sky is blue in Tucson all the time," he replied.

She dished two eggs from the cast-iron frying pan and put two pieces of bacon on the plate. She turned and set it down in front of him.

"Over easy? My favorite, what's the occasion?" he

asked.

"Do I need an occasion to make you over easy? They're your favorite," she said.

"Yes, they're my favorite, but you hardly ever make them. You normally just give me regular fried eggs," he reminded her.

She dished herself breakfast and quickly took a seat next to him. "I was thinking."

He put his fork down and said, "Here it comes. So the over-easy eggs was bribery?"

"I was thinking about that sermon you made a couple of weeks ago," she said.

His curiosity piqued, he asked, "Which one?"

"Joshua 1:9," she replied.

With a broad smile he recited, "Have I not commanded you? Be strong and courageous. Do not be frightened, and do not be dismayed, for the Lord your God is with you wherever you go."

"Yes, that one. And I was thinking that yesterday God intervened and saved my life. I don't think that's an accident. He has a purpose for me, and that's to go to Prescott."

"Wait, no, hold on," Benedict said, shaking his head.

"I must not allow evil men to stop me from fulfilling God's plan," she said defensively.

"No, never happening," Benedict said firmly.

"I can ask John Smith to accompany me, and if you want, you can hire another gunman to join us," she said.

"No."

"But it's my purpose," she insisted.

"I said NO!" he blared.

"Daddy, I'm not a little girl, I'm a woman now. The children need me, and I must go to them. If I don't, then the bandits won."

"No, and that's final," he declared.

"This is my purpose. I was saved so I could make the trip. God has a purpose for me, I can see it," Katherine said.

Benedict slammed his fist down and barked, "No, and that's it. No more talk about Prescott, the children, traveling, ever, you hear me?"

"But—" she said.

"No buts. Your place is not in an orphanage, it's here with me. Now listen, I won't hear another word about it. Do you understand?" he blared.

Defeated, Katherine lowered her head and just above a whisper said, "Yes, sir."

"And that John Smith, he's not welcome here anymore. I'm thankful for what he did, but it's time for him to go. I won't hear any challenges to my authority. He's gone. When he returns, you're to direct him to me and I'll inform him. Do you understand?"

"Yes, sir," Katherine said, her head still down.

Benedict looked at his half-eaten plate. He'd lost his appetite. He got up from the table and marched out of the room. "I have to go to the church. I'll be back in a few hours."

\*\*\*

Daniels and John spent the morning going over the plan. Being a trusting man, Daniels included his two deputies, Garrett and Wheeler, because if this was going to be successful, he needed them on board.

At first, Garrett and Wheeler were leery of the idea but were quickly persuaded.

With the plan set, all they needed was nightfall to come. Hungry and knowing he'd need some rest before the long night, John headed back to the Rawles residence.

He was walking past the Gem Saloon when a man hollered his *real* name. "Nichols!" John kept walking, pretending he didn't hear his name being called.

"Nichols, John Nichols, is that you?" a man yelled as he exited the saloon and ran after John.

John kept acting like he didn't hear him.

The man caught up and began to walk beside John. "Corporal Nichols, is it you?"

"I don't know who you're referring to," John lied.

The man stepped in front of John and held out his arm. "It's me, Private Jackson." Jackson was thin, his face gaunt and clothes tattered. He staggered backwards two steps and again said, "It's me, Private Jackson."

John did recognize him, but he couldn't risk blowing his cover. A tinge of sympathy ran through him as he looked at his fellow compatriot and saw the man had fallen on hard times. "I don't know a Private Jackson."

"Corporal Nichols, it's me," Jackson said, his jovial tone replaced with disappointment and sorrow.

"You're a drunk. Get out of my way," John said and pushed past him.

Jackson turned and called out, "Corporal Nichols, why? How could you turn your back on a fellow soldier? Everything we went through. Is it because of the way I'm dressed? Huh? Are you too fancy and upstanding to be seen with me? You don't want your Yankee friends to look down on you?"

John pressed forward. The barbs against him stung, but everything was about a means to an end.

"Some son of the South you are! You see a brother in need and you spit on them. Well, guess what? I spit on you!" Jackson yelled and spit. His loud and verbose behavior was catching the eyes of many who walked by. One person who saw the scene was Mr. Geist. He was leaning against a railing in front of his bar and saw the entire scene unfold. Recognizing John from earlier, he wanted to see if this drunkard had any information that could be valuable. He tossed the cigarette he'd been smoking and strutted over to Jackson, who was still yelling and screaming in the direction John had gone.

"Hello, fine sir," Geist said, stopping a few feet away from Jackson.

Jackson spun around quickly, almost falling over due to his inebriated condition. "What do you want?"

"Just to talk," Geist said.

Jackson looked at Geist from head to toe. "Aren't you a proper gentleman with your polished leather shoes and finely pressed suit."

"How about I buy you a drink or two?"

"A drink? I think I might be convinced, but what do you want?" Jackson asked.

"Just to talk," he replied. He turned and pointed back to his bar. "You see that establishment?"

"Yeah, they have good games of chance and the women are pretty, but their damn whiskey is watered down," Jackson said.

"Watered down? I'd disagree with you, but how about we go there and I buy you a drink."

"Buy me one at the Gem instead," Jackson said.

"I'd prefer we go to the Bella Grande on account that I own it."

"You own the Bella? Well, what do you know? Since you're the owner, how about you give me a special on one of your ladies?" Jackson proposed.

Geist turned, pointed to the Bella Grande and said, "We can discuss incentives like that, but it all depends on what you can share with me. So, do we have an arrangement?"

"You just want to talk?"

"I have a few questions about the man you were just with. Do you think you can answer those?" Geist asked.

Seeing an opportunity to leverage more, Jackson said, "I'll tell you anything you want to know about that backstabbing son of a bitch, but it might cost you more than a drink."

"We can discuss terms. Now, if you'll follow me, let's get you a drink," Geist said.

\*\*\*

John entered the Rawles residence and walked right into Katherine, who looked upset. "Are you okay?"

"Yes, I'm fine, thank you for asking," she said, tucking a few loose strands of hair behind her ear.

"I want to thank you again for allowing me to stay here. Your generosity will always be remembered," John said.

"You're quite welcome," she replied sheepishly.

Unable to walk away without knowing what was troubling her, he pressed again, "Something vexes you; please tell me. If I can help, I'd do whatever I could."

Katherine went to talk but cut herself short. She turned away from him and was about to step away when he touched her arm.

"Katherine, please, if something is troubling you, please let me know," John said.

She faced him, and just as she was opening her mouth to speak, the front door opened and in came Benedict.

Benedict saw John touching Katherine's arm and instantly became hostile. "Get your filthy hands off her!"

John quickly removed his hand and turned to face Benedict. "It's not what you think. She's upset and was just sharing what concerned her."

"With you? Why would she do that? She met you just yesterday. We know nothing about you or why you're really in Tucson."

"I can see you're very upset, but I can assure you my

intentions here are nothing you or Katherine should be concerned about."

"How do I know that?" Benedict barked and took a couple of steps towards John.

Seeing his temper was flared and not wanting to get into an altercation that he couldn't take back, John lowered his voice and calmly replied, "You're absolutely right to be wary of a stranger. If I were you, I'd be the same way. How about I just go to the bedroom, collect my items and leave?"

"Daddy, this isn't fair. He didn't do anything," Katherine protested.

"Katherine, be quiet. This doesn't concern you," Benedict said.

"Oh, but it does," she fired back. It was unusual for her to respond like she did, but she couldn't allow what she perceived as an injustice against John to stand without objection.

"I won't say it again, Katherine, leave the room. This is a discussion between two men," Benedict roared.

She flared her nostrils and marched out of the room.

Benedict turned to John and ordered, "Go upstairs, get your things and leave."

John merely nodded and said, "Yes, sir."

***

The sounds of laughter, conversation and game playing filled the air of the Bella Grande. Geist was proud of his establishment, but his ambition was greater than the four walls around him. He knew if he was to become the great and wealthy man he desired, he'd need the land to the north because there he planned on developing a depot for the future train service he knew was coming. The only things that stood in his way were the current owner and Sheriff Daniels, who was preventing him from acquiring it all because Daniels wouldn't exercise the eviction notice because the owners had managed to get an appeal through the court.

Geist poured Jackson another shot of whiskey in the hopes that Jackson would provide more information than he had about John. "That's it? He's just a former Confederate soldier?"

"Is that not enough?" Jackson said before tossing back the shot.

"How does he know Sheriff Daniels?"

"I didn't know he did," Jackson said, pushing his empty glass towards Geist.

Geist pulled the bottle away, inserted the cork and said, "Bar's closed for free drinks."

"But I can tell you more about Corporal Nichols. He, um, he once shot a prisoner, yep, shot the poor man dead after he'd surrendered to us," Jackson said, his voice slurring.

"I don't care about what he did during the war. I need to know more about his relationship with the sheriff."

"I, um, I can find out. I could be like one of them Pinkerton fellas but just work for you," Jackson proposed.

"No, it doesn't appear your old comrade has any information worth knowing," Geist said, standing up.

"Um, how about this? I go follow him, see, and if he does, you then can pay me, huh?" Jackson asked.

Geist thought about the idea; he liked it. "I think we can make that arrangement work."

"Ahh, is it possible I can get an advance?" Jackson asked, his eyes on the bottle in Geist's grip.

"If you come back with some very good information that links your friend with Sheriff Daniels, something valuable, I'll give you a case of whiskey," Geist offered.

Jackson's face sagged with disappointment.

"I suggest you go to work," Geist said before being interrupted by a burly man who whispered in his ear. Geist frowned and said loudly, "I don't give a shit what that bitch says; if a paying customer wants something, she gives it to him. Tell her to do it or she's gone, period."

The man nodded and rushed off.

Geist watched Jackson stumble out of the Bella Grande. His level of trust in his accomplishing his task was low, but if he could get something on Daniels he could leverage against him, it was worth employing the town drunk.

# CHAPTER FIVE

*"My failures have been errors in judgment, not of intent."*
— Ulysses S. Grant

TUCSON, ARIZONA TERRITORY

JULY 18, 1876

A single gunshot woke John. He sat up and looked around the dark hotel room.

A cool breeze gently blew in through the open window, carrying with it the sounds of the rowdy streets of Tucson.

His ears searched for something that would explain the gunfire, but nothing came. *Is a man dead on the ground? Or was some drunk fool just celebrating a win at the baccarat table?* Whatever it was, no other shots followed.

John found a box of matches on the nightstand and lit one. The dim orange glow of the match allowed him to see his small and sparsely furnished room. He touched the flame to the wick of a candle, and soon the light grew in strength. Curious as to the time, he opened his pocket watch to find his first official shift would be starting soon.

A knock on the door gave him an uneasy feeling. "Yes!"

"Excuse me, sir, this is the hotel manager. You requested I knock on your door at this hour," a man replied.

"Yes, thank you," John said.

"Will you be needing anything else, sir?"

"No," John answered.

"Very well, sir, have a good night," the man said and walked off. His heavy footfalls sounded in the hall.

John got out of bed, stretched and went to the washbasin in the far corner of the room. He filled the bowl and splashed the cool water on his face. He looked at his reflection in the mirror. On his face he looked at the deep wrinkles etched around his eyes. He was satisfied that his scheme was progressing with ease, but after spending eleven years tracking down Pruitt's men, he was accustomed to obstacles and hardship and knew that tonight he was embarking on something that could easily go off the rails. A tinge of fear crept into his thoughts, fear that he'd get killed. This wasn't a fear born of a desire to live, but one from dying before he could fulfill his purpose. The thought of Pruitt outliving him was dreadful to ponder. Never before had he gone up against someone as well armed and protected as the Captain. It was a huge risk, but one he needed to take if he were to find and kill the one man ultimately responsible for his family's death.

Knocking at his door pulled him from his thoughts. He toweled his face off and called out, "Yes."

"It's the sheriff," Daniels replied.

John unlocked and flung the door open. "Evening, Sheriff."

Daniels walked into the room and closed the door. "You sure you want to do this?"

"Yes, I'm sure."

"Okay, me and the other deputies will be located just down the street just in case something goes wrong," Daniels said.

"Sheriff, just make sure you're not spotted. Try to look natural. I don't want to have him get spooked. This plan only works if he thinks no one is trailing him."

"I understand."

John put on his shirt and boots and wrapped his gun belt around his waist. He picked up his rifle and headed for the door. "I hope to be back by dawn with word on their hideout."

"Hey, Johnny Reb," Daniels said.

John stopped short of leaving. He turned to face Daniels and said, "Yes."

"Here, you'll need this," Daniels said, holding a deputy's badge in the palm of his hand.

John picked it up. A slight grin graced his face. He'd never imagined he would be a full-fledged sheriff's deputy, yet here he was. He pinned the badge to his wool vest and exited the room.

\*\*\*

To play the role of an incompetent deputy, John had brought props with him. The second Garrett left him in charge of the office, John removed a whiskey bottle from a satchel and placed it on the desk. He pulled the cork, poured a tall glass, took a drink and loudly declared, "Praise the Lord. Whiskey is proof that God truly loves us."

Ferguson sat up in his cell and looked at John. "Hey, Deputy, you got enough to share?"

John cocked his head and said with a thick Georgia drawl, "With an outlaw? I don't think so."

"Where you from?" Ferguson asked.

"Georgia, now shut your mouth," John replied honestly.

"What's a son of the South doing all the way out here?" Ferguson asked, now standing near the bars, his eyes longingly staring at the bottle of whiskey.

The other day, John had picked up on a slight accent in Ferguson's voice and hoped to garner rapport. "Seemed like a nice place to settle down."

"Did you fight in the war?" Ferguson asked.

"I thought I told you to shut your mouth," John growled then took a drink.

"I, um, was with the Fifth Tennessee. I fought at Shiloh and Chickamauga."

John took a long drink, looked at Ferguson and asked, "Was it as bad as they say at Chickamauga?"

"Worse, if you ask me. I was wounded and captured. I spent the next year and a half at Point Lookout in Maryland as a prisoner of war. It was dreadful, downright miserable conditions. I'm lucky to have survived it."

"And now look at you," John mocked.

"C'mon, how about you share some of that whiskey? I might be hanging by the end of the day tomorrow. Look kindly on a fella compatriot of the Cause."

"On one condition," John bartered.

"What's that?"

"You answer some questions," John said.

Ferguson looked up and to the left as he quickly pondered. A smile broke his grizzled face. "Deal. Now bring me a tall glass."

John grabbed another glass and filled it halfway. He walked over and handed it to him. He lifted his glass and went to seal what he hoped was a bit of trust. "Here's to the Cause. May the South rise again."

"May she rise again," Ferguson said, clanging his glass against John's and letting out a rebel yell before swigging the entire contents of the glass. "Hot damn, that's good whiskey." He handed the glass back to John. "A bit more?"

"First question, and this is just my curiosity asking, but why do you call yourself Watch Eye?"

"Start with the easy questions." Ferguson laughed. He took a drink and finally answered, "On account I have one blue eye and one brown."

"Interesting," John mused.

"More," Ferguson pleaded, his arm extended through the bars.

John took his glass and set it on the desk and took a seat. "No more until you tell me what brought you out here all the way from Tennessee."

Ferguson sat on his cot. "Opportunity. I went home to Paris, but the place wasn't the same. Most of the young men had either been killed or never came back. There was a heavy dark cloud that hung over it. Many of the shops were closed, and the mill was shut down, leaving most of us without work. A friend from childhood told me about opportunities in the Southwest. He told me there were large expanses of land just ready to be settled. That's all I needed to hear. I was gone the next week and rode until I reached this dusty little town. The funny thing was I was too late, what land had been set aside was taken by Yankee officers, bankers and the like. I quickly found myself down on my luck with no place to call home…" he said before pausing.

"You okay?" John asked.

"Fill up my glass," Ferguson replied, getting up and walking to the bars. He extended his arm through and waved the empty glass.

"Why would a Tennessee boy run with a Union captain?" John asked, walking towards the cell.

"Fill it up and I'll tell you," he replied.

John poured more whiskey.

Ferguson took a drink, paused and answered, "I was a man without a home. The Captain gave that to me and gave me something that I had lost a long time ago."

"What's that?" John asked, genuinely curious.

"Purpose," Ferguson answered with sincerity.

"Who is he?" John asked.

Ferguson finished the glass and put his arm out again.

John half-filled it.

Ferguson took a big gulp and replied, "I don't know anything about him. There's rumors, but no one really knows who he is."

"Is he from New York?"

Ferguson cut his eyes at John and said, "You're hoping to ply me with booze in hopes that I'll spill the beans on the one man who's ever given a shit about me." He turned his glass upside down and let the contents pour onto the floor.

John smiled and went back to the desk. "More for me."

***

A couple of quiet hours passed by. John filled the time with cards while Ferguson lay in his cell sleeping. The hope had been he'd get some information from him with the whiskey. He'd gotten some, but nothing that helped identify the Captain. With that phase of his plan ending in failure, he'd have to move on to phase two.

The front door of the office opened and in walked a young and attractive woman. She walked over to John and straddled him on the chair. "Good evening, sugar."

"Good evening…I thought I told you I was working," John said, playing the role.

"You did, but I couldn't wait until morning. How about we go somewhere?" she purred in his ear.

Ferguson woke and caught sight of the woman. Curious, he sat up and watched the interaction between the two like a voyeur.

The woman seductively ran her fingers through John's hair and began to move her hips.

John was playing a role, but he was struggling not to get truly excited. Out of the corner of his eye, he spotted

Ferguson watching them. Now was the time to fully execute phase two with hopes Ferguson would take the bait. "Just stop, hold on."

The woman stopped and complained, "What's wrong?"

"It's not you, it's these damn things," John said, removing the loop of keys for the sheriff's office from his belt loop. He tossed them onto the edge of the desk nearest the cell and immediately started kissing the woman.

Ferguson stared at the keys.

The woman stopped kissing, pulled back and said, "I can't do this with him watching like a deviant. Can we go out back?"

John nodded.

The two got up and headed outside, leaving the keys on the desk.

Ferguson continued to stare at the keys. They were out of arm's reach, but if he could fashion something, he just might be able to get them. Without hesitation he ripped the sheets off the cot and tied one end around a boot. He leaned as far as he could through the bars and tossed the boot. The first attempt failed as the boot hit the side of the desk. He tried again, and this time the boot landed on top of the desk just past the keys. He slowly tugged to confirm the boot was secured tight. Seeing it was, he pulled hard. The boot caught the keys and threw them onto the floor and within his reach. He grabbed them and quickly unlocked the door to the cell.

Knowing he didn't have long, he put his boot back

on and went to the rifle rack but found it locked. Remembering he had a set of keys, he grabbed them but found that none of the keys worked. "Damn," he growled. If he was going to escape, he'd have to just leave. He gave up on trying to get a firearm and headed out the front door.

The street in front of the office was quiet, no one around except a lone horse hitched a few feet away. He untied the horse, jumped on its back and raced off towards the north.

The entire time Ferguson was working on his escape, John was spying through a hole in the wall. When he saw him exit, he went to Molly, which he had hitched up out back, and quickly took off in pursuit. The pitch black of night was perfect for concealment but made it extremely difficult to keep sight of his target. As he rode out of town and into the immense dark, he prayed this plan would prove to be the right one.

\*\*\*

Pursuing Ferguson wasn't as easy as John had imagined it would be. The pitch black of night made it almost impossible. However, with a combination of skill and luck, he kept on his trail until Ferguson stopped at what appeared to be an abandoned shack in the mountains. Ensuring he wouldn't be noticed, John kept his distance. Using his ears more than his eyes, he heard a door creak open then slam shut. Believing Ferguson was inside and it was safe to move, he did. Swiftly he got off Molly and ran towards the shack.

The sound of the door opening made John leap towards cover near a watering trough. Heavy footfalls were followed by the door slamming again. Feeling he was safe, John looked up, but it was difficult to see anything except for the dim glow coming from inside the shack, no doubt from a lantern or candle. Needing to know if anyone else was with Ferguson, John got to his feet and hurried towards the shack to get a look inside. He reached the far side, about ten feet from the front door, and he found a crack in between the wood siding and peeked inside. All he could see was a table, three chairs and a single lantern burning, but no sign of Ferguson or anyone else.

"Psst," Ferguson said, standing behind John.

John reached for his pistol and turned, but he was unable to make the full turn. Ferguson struck him with the handle of a pickax. John absorbed the first blow, but the second sent him reeling backwards. John fell against the side of the shack.

Ferguson came down a third time, but John blocked it with his arm. A fortunate move by him 'cause had he not, it would have hit him in the head. Ferguson raised the handle, but this time John didn't just wait to get hit. He lunged from his position, wrapped his arms around Ferguson's waist and tackled him to the ground. With Ferguson on his back, John straddled him and began to level punches against him; however, Ferguson still held on to the handle and used it, this time jabbing John under his rib cage on the left. John recoiled from the pain, giving Ferguson another opportunity to jab and he did. This time the handle made solid contact against his head. John fell back and hit the ground. Ferguson scrambled to his feet, lifted the handle and swung down several more times. On the second strike, John could hear his ribs break. He grunted in pain. He knew something had to change or he'd be dead. Knowing he still had his pistol, he reached down, pulled the Colt from its holster, cocked it and pulled the trigger just as Ferguson was coming down with another blow.

The round struck Ferguson in the chest. He stumbled backwards but still held onto the handle.

John cocked the pistol again and fired. He repeated this two more times.

Ferguson dropped to his knees and fell face forward into the dirt. By the time his head hit, he was dead.

John rolled onto his side and tried to get up, but an electrical jolt of pain shot through his body. He rolled onto his back and lay for a second. He knew he had to get up. He didn't know the extent of his injuries, but there was no doubt he was in bad shape. "Get up, John. Get up," he said out loud. He grunted loudly as he tried again, the pain was shooting all over his body, but there was no way he'd allow himself to just lie there. Using brute determination and willpower, he got to his feet. A forceful sensation of vertigo began to wash over him as he walked towards Molly. He lost his balance and fell to his knees. "Get up!" he said again, this time loudly. He slowly got to his feet, but this time he made calculated steps, ensuring each footfall was firmly placed. He did this for what seemed like an eternity until he reached Molly. Using his last bit of energy, he mounted Molly and headed for the one place he knew he'd find comfort, Katherine's house.

\*\*\*

Katherine walked into the kitchen, and to her surprise she found Benedict sitting at the table with his hands clasped together. "Oh, good morning," she said.

"Good morning. Please take a seat," he said, nodding to an empty chair across from him.

Katherine did as he said. A wave of nervous energy washed through her, as she rarely saw him so subdued. She sat and placed her hands in her lap.

"I've given a lot of thought to the incident yesterday morning with Mr. Smith, and I wanted to offer my apologies to you. I was a bit harsh, and for that I'm truly sorry. I know you would never do or allow someone to do something improper. I can only explain my actions stem from old wounds from the war that have never healed."

She took his hand in hers and said, "I know you love me and you always have my best interest at heart."

"I prayed much over the incident, and I feel foolish. I should never conduct myself with such anger. I allowed hate to dominate my thoughts."

"I'm happy to hear you took comfort in prayer."

"Can you forgive me?" he asked sheepishly.

Her eyes widened and she said, "Why, of course.

Like I said, I know you love me, and nothing you've ever done would ever shake my love and gratefulness for you. No one is perfect, isn't that what you often say?"

He nodded.

"All we can do is strive to be like Jesus. We will falter, but we must ask for forgiveness and get back up and keep moving forward," she said confidently.

"You're so wise. I venture to say you're becoming wiser than me. I may need to start looking to you for guidance," he said, gently squeezing her hand.

"Shall I make you breakfast?" she asked, trying to pull away, but he wouldn't let her go.

"I have one other thing to tell you."

She sat and listened intently.

"You put forth a proposition yesterday morning, and once more, after thought and much prayer, I've decided to allow you to go to Prescott. You are right, God has a purpose for you, and that begins with those children."

"Oh, Daddy, are you serious? Am I dreaming right now?" she said, her tone rising a couple of decibels. "I need to run to the telegraph office straight away and let them know in Prescott. Oh, how they'll be so happy to know I'm coming. Daddy, you've made me the happiest daughter, thank you."

"There's one condition," he said bluntly.

Her tone mellowed out. "What's the condition?"

"We're going together."

"I don't understand," she said, her face contorted in confusion.

"I've been in Tucson for a long time, we both have.

You're the only family I have, and while you've been with me on my journey to create a thriving congregation, it's my turn to travel with you and support what you want now. I hear Prescott is beautiful, and they could always use a new pastor."

Unsure how to act, she sat and thought.

"You look vexed," he said.

"I don't understand why you'd walk away from your congregation and go with me. You've worked so hard for so many years."

"Call it a compromise. You want to pursue a passion, and I won't let you go alone. So that leaves us with two options. You stay with me here, or I go with you. It's not fair for me to hold you back, but I can't allow you to go out on that road without me. So I'll travel with you to Prescott, get you settled in, and I may stay or I may come back to Tucson if you don't need me there and I know you're safe."

A broad smile stretched across her face. "Thank you."

"You're welcome. Now how about some eggs and bacon?"

She happily jumped up from the table and began to prepare breakfast.

\*\*\*

Garrett climbed off his horse. His legs, back and shoulders ached from the hours of hard riding.

Daniels exited the sheriff's office and blared, "Well,

did you find him?"

Garrett removed his wide-brimmed hat and shook his head, a frown telling Daniels of his disappointment.

"Let's see what Wheeler finds," Daniels said.

"Nothing," Garrett said.

"You've seen Wheeler?" Daniels asked.

"He took his horse to Talon's Stables. He's swapping for a fresh horse and riding out again," Garrett informed him.

Daniels sighed. His deputies had ridden after John left in pursuit of the bandit but lost track of him on the outskirts of town. Through the night and morning, they continued looking for him or the bandit, but neither could be found.

"I need rest; then I'll turn around and head back out," Garrett said.

"Good man," Daniels said.

Hollering echoed from down the street.

Daniels looked and saw it was Geist followed by a small entourage. "Sheriff Daniels here lost their prisoner, I hear!"

A look of shock appeared on both Garrett's and Daniels' faces.

Geist walked up and shouted, "Everyone listen here. The sheriff arrested one of Captain's Raiders and in no time allowed the criminal to escape. Is that incompetence? I say so!"

Passersby slowed and took notice. Many began to talk amongst themselves and point at Daniels.

"What do you have to say to the people of Tucson?"

Geist asked.

"Want me to run them off?" Garrett asked.

"No, go rest. I won't subject myself to this," Daniels said. He turned around and walked into his office. Geist's howls and accusations continued. Daniels sat behind his desk and pondered his next step. Just how fast word had gotten out about the escaped bandit came as a surprise. A myriad of questions rushed into his mind. *Who told? Did someone witness the escape? What am I going to do about it?* And finally. *Where is John?*

Geist was taking great joy at Daniels' expense. He'd been trying to find a way to get back at him, and now, without a doubt, he had found one, and all at Daniels' own hand, but if he was going to ensure he buried Daniels, he needed to go for the proverbial kill shot. He turned to one of his men and said, "Go find that drunk Jackson. I've got another job for him."

# CHAPTER SIX

"Learn from your mistakes and build on your successes."
– John C. Calhoun

## TUCSON, ARIZONA TERRITORY

## JULY 19, 1876

Katherine was excited about Benedict changing his mind; what she didn't expect was he'd make arrangements so quickly. Benedict had booked them on the Overland for a departure tomorrow morning. This meant she'd be spending the time in between once more preparing for the long trip. So much had happened in such a short period of time, it made her head spin a little.

A loud thump followed by a crash sounded from the front porch.

She walked to her bedroom window, which overlooked the front yard, and expected to see Benedict, but she saw nothing. Benedict had ridden into town to gather a few items for the trip, so if it wasn't him, who was it?

She walked slowly down the stairs but saw no one or anything unusual through the front bay window. Cautiously she went to a small window near the front door, pulled the curtain aside and peered out. Lying on the front porch was John, and he looked bad. She threw open the door and rushed out. "John, oh no, what happened?"

John could barely open his swollen and puffy eyes. Small deep cuts were all over his bloodied face.

"John, can you walk?" she asked, trying to lift his head into her lap.

He mumbled something unintelligible.

The neigh of a horse drew her attention towards the barn. There she saw Molly wandering.

"Water," he said barely above a whisper.

"Yes, water. You rest here. I'll be right back," she said, gently laying his head on the porch and running off. She returned with a glass and a wet cloth. She lifted his head and put the glass of cool water to his scabbed lips.

He sipped a small amount of water then began to cough.

"Take it easy, small sips," she said.

He tried to sip again, but it only resulted in a coughing fit.

"What happened to you?"

He lay without responding.

The sound of a wagon came from down the drive.

Katherine looked and saw Benedict riding up. Based upon his last encounter, he wondered how Benedict would handle this.

Seeing Katherine on the porch with a man in her arms, Benedict whipped the horses to get to her as fast as he could. When he arrived, he leapt from the wagon and ran to her. "What happened?"

"I don't know. I heard a noise out front. I came to investigate and found him lying here just like this," she replied.

"We need to contact the sheriff," Benedict said.

"Yes, sheriff," John muttered.

"Daddy, help me get him inside; then go get the sheriff," Katherine urged.

Benedict hesitated for a second then acted. He scooped John up and carried him to the spare bedroom upstairs. Once he was placed in the bed, he turned to Katherine. "Care for him. I'll return with the sheriff and a doctor."

"Okay," Katherine said.

Benedict sprinted down the stairs, out to his wagon and hurried off.

Katherine looked down at a badly wounded John and wondered what she should do first. It made sense to remove some of his clothing, but was that the proper thing to do? She bent down and began to unbutton his vest then stopped when doubt popped in her mind. What would Father think if he came back and John was half dressed? Would he be upset? But what if she did nothing? He lay there motionless, his breathing shallow. "Think," she said out loud. Finding the courage to do what was right, she began to undress him. She removed his vest, then unbuttoned his shirt to find large bruises all over, with one large dark purple bruise on his side. She took a wet cloth and began to wipe the dried blood from his face, neck and hands, being careful not to tear open any scabs.

As she tenderly wiped his arms, he began to stir. He turned his head and opened his eyes to mere slits. "Thank you."

"Don't talk, just rest."

He reached over and took her hand in his. "I had nowhere to go…but here."

"I'm happy you thought of us. Now close your eyes and sleep. Daddy went to fetch the sheriff and the doctor."

"I need to talk to the sheriff. I…" John said but stopped when he began to cough. He grimaced in pain with each deep cough.

"You don't listen well. Don't talk. There will be plenty of time to talk later," she said sternly.

He settled down from the coughing fit and melted into the thick down pillow.

"Daddy says men are trouble. I can see what he means," she quipped.

\*\*\*

Doc Evers exited John's room to find Benedict, Katherine and Daniels anxiously waiting there. "He's been badly beaten, his left ribs are broken, he has eight deep lacerations, a lot of bruising, and he's dehydrated. It looks like he took quite the beating. It's amazing he found his way back."

"He'll live?" Katherine asked, a clear tone of concern in her voice.

"Heavens yes. All he needs is lots of rest. I wrapped his torso, just monitor that. I left an ointment to put on it that will help soothe the area, and I also left a bottle of laudanum for his pain. Give him a tablespoon every few hours. If you need more, just let me know."

Katherine nodded.

"Can we see him?" Daniels asked.

"He's awake, but don't get him too excited. He needs his rest," Doc Evers warned.

Daniels turned to Benedict. "Give me some privacy with him."

Benedict nodded.

Daniels ignored the suggestion from Evers and went into the room, closing the door behind him. "Johnny Reb, what the hell happened?"

John was sitting up, propped up by several pillows. His face was swollen and he could barely open his eyes. "I followed him to an old shack, or that's what it looked like. It was hard to see. He went in and I waited. Next thing I know, I got hit over the head. Somehow he exited the shack and snuck up behind me. After he hit me in the head, he began to pummel me. I can only guess it was a big stick, a handle to a pickax or something. I lost count of how many times he hit me. I managed to pull my pistol and shoot him dead. How I got to Molly is a blur. Next thing I know, I'm outside here," John explained.

"So he's dead?" Daniels asked.

"Yeah."

"And you didn't see anyone else?"

"No, but like I said, it was dark out."

"Can you show me or at least tell me where this shack is located?" Daniels asked.

"Yeah, I think so." John grimaced in pain as he sat up straighter.

"Where were you?"

"Northwest of town, in the hills about six maybe seven miles. He took a beaten trail; it was rocky. The shack looked like it might have had something to do with a mine."

"I think I know where you might have been," Daniels said. "You get some rest."

"I'm sorry," John said.

"I'm the one who's sorry. I wish I had never allowed you to talk me into this harebrained idea." Daniels sighed. He fiddled with his hat and continued, "I'll come back and check on you in a few days."

"Very well. As soon as I can, I'll come back to work," John said.

"You just rest for now. We'll talk about your position later," Daniels said and promptly walked out, leaving the door open.

Benedict stepped in and closed the door. "John, how are you feeling?"

"I've seen better days, sir."

"What happened?" Benedict asked, pulling a chair over and placing it next to the bed. He sat down and crossed his legs.

"I was attacked by the man we found the other day. I was deputized by Sheriff Daniels, and on my first night working, the prisoner escaped. I pursued and, well, as you can see, it didn't work out for me, although I did manage to kill him."

"I see, hmm," Benedict said, running his fingers through his mustache. "I suppose you'll be needing a place to convalesce?"

"I know I'm not welcome here. If I can get some help, I'll go back to my hotel and rest there," John offered.

"No, that won't be necessary. What kind of man of God would I be if I tossed out a wounded man? No, you'll be staying; but the thing is I'll have to hire you a caretaker, as I'm taking Katherine to Prescott tomorrow on the eight o'clock coach—"

The door burst open. "Daddy, we're staying. Prescott can wait. We can't leave Mr. Smith here like this with some stranger looking after him. God sent him to our door, and it's our responsibility to care for him."

"But, Katherine—"

"No, I'm insisting. When he gets better, you and I will go, but not a day sooner," she said defiantly.

Benedict sank into his chair. He wanted to protest but couldn't find the courage to do it now. "Let me leave you, then. I need to go to the Overland and reschedule and have them send a telegraph to Prescott."

"Thank you, Daddy," Katherine said, proud that she'd stood her ground and had been victorious.

"I don't feel good about this arrangement. If you're scheduled to leave—"

She interrupted him and snapped, "Not a peep out of you. Get some rest."

"Let me—"

"No, not another word. Rest is what you need. Now lie down. I'll be back up here in a couple of hours to give you your medicine," she said and marched out of the room, closing the door behind her.

John couldn't believe he was in this situation and wanted nothing more than to get up and leave, but the pain that racked his entire body was too much to overcome. He slid down into the warm sheets and closed his eyes.

# CHAPTER SEVEN

"Beware the wrath of a patient adversary." – John C. Calhoun

TUCSON, ARIZONA TERRITORY

JULY 22, 1876

John woke to chatter downstairs. Curious, he slowly rose from the bed and walked to the door. He opened it and stuck his head out to get a better listen.

Down in the kitchen, Katherine and Benedict were debating rescheduling the trip to Prescott.

By the sound of the conversation, John could tell Benedict was ready to leave, but Katherine was pushing to remain until he was better. He hated being a thorn in their side and could understand why Benedict wanted to get on with his life. However, he had been enjoying the past couple of days at the house. Katherine had proven to be a doting caretaker. During her visits, they would often spend many minutes just talking. For him, he hadn't felt a connection with someone for a long time until Katherine. There was something familiar, she reminded him of his wife, Elizabeth; but for the similarities there were also differences. Where Elizabeth tended to be timid, Katherine had an edge to her. She still respected Benedict and would relent to his desires, but she would make sure her thoughts were expressed. He liked and respected that about her. He didn't want to use the word *love*, but he was

94

definitely growing fond of her. When she'd leave his room, he lay and thought about her; but quickly he'd put any thoughts of them being together out of his mind. He was twelve years her senior, he had nothing to offer her, and more importantly, he had a mission to accomplish.

Hearing their conversation turn to the chores of the day, John grew bored and closed the door. He shuffled back to the bed and laid down. The beating he'd taken the other night was the worst he'd ever been hurt. He was a tough man and had been through a lot, but never had his body received such abuse.

A tap on the door came.

"Yes, come in," he called out.

The door creaked open and in came Katherine. As usual she was wearing a gentle smile and this morning carried a tray full of food, no doubt eggs, bacon and biscuits, the typical but much-appreciated breakfast.

He sat up and smoothed out the sheet and blanket.

Katherine placed the tray on his lap and said, "There you go, over medium, and the bacon cooked crisp."

He reached towards the glass of milk and accidentally touched her hand. She didn't move hers, nor did he retract. He looked up and saw she was returning his gaze. "Ahh, thank you. You're the best. I don't know what I'd do without you."

Just before she pulled her hand back, her smile melted away to an expression he'd never seen. "Oh, well, um, it's what good Christian people do, and it's my way of showing you how grateful I am for you saving me."

"You never had to repay me, but if everything you've

done for me is that, it's too much. I don't know how I'll ever equal your and Benedict's hospitality and generosity."

"It's our pleasure," she said, pulling a chair up so she could sit down.

Seeing the chair, he grew happy, as it meant she'd be spending some time with him. He dug into his eggs and filled his mouth with a forkful of it and the bacon.

"Tell me more about Alabama," she said.

"What would you like to know?" he asked. A wave of guilt washed over him, as he hated lying to her. Yes, he knew it was best he do so; but now he convinced himself that it was to protect her.

"You may think this question inappropriate, but did you ever own slaves?"

"First, the question isn't inappropriate, and second, no, I did not. In fact, many a Southerner didn't own slaves. The vast majority of slaves were held by the few wealthy plantation or commercial enterprise owners."

"I've read that all white Southerners owned Negros," she said.

"That's just false. I actually worked closely with them, as I was a tenant farmer."

"What is a tenant farmer?"

"We lease land from a plantation owner and work the land with hopes our crops return a profit."

She looked out the window and sighed. "It's so brown and dead here. I hear the South is lush and green. I so miss the big oaks and tall grasses of Ohio."

"Now I have a question that may be inappropriate

and, dare I say, personal."

"Please go ahead. If it is inappropriate, I'll tell you, but not one question you've ever asked has been that, so I trust this won't be."

"The first night I was here, you said you were from Ohio and Benedict was from Pennsylvania. The way you worded it was odd."

She looked down and began to fiddle with a loose piece of thread from her apron.

Seeing her composure had shifted, he said, "I apologize. I can see what I said was definitely inappropriate. Please forgive me."

"No, no, it wasn't; in fact, it's a normal and perfectly reasonable question to ask based upon what you heard. I'll be honest, I don't know why Daddy got upset. You see, he adopted me; well, before he did that, he saved me from a band of bloodthirsty Apaches. I had been with my birth family. We were coming to Tucson for new opportunities when we came under attack. They killed my parents, but before they could get to me, Benedict came down like an angel sent from God and saved me. He's raised me since that day, and I consider him a father as if he were my blood. He's a good man. I'm blessed he's in my life; I just wish I could help him with his nightmares," she said.

Picking up on the last comment, John asked, "Nightmares? Does he have them often?"

A panicked look spread across her face. "Oh, I shouldn't have said that. Please forget I even mentioned it."

Not wishing to upset her, he said, "I won't say a word, I promise."

"He'd lock me in my room for a year if he knew I said that," she said.

"It's okay, I swear I won't repeat what you said, but I do have a question concerning what he did before he came out here."

"He doesn't talk much about it."

"Nothing?"

"Just that he doesn't like people from the South, and it's all because of what he saw during the war."

"He fought in the war?"

"Yes. But I don't know what he did during the war. He doesn't share anything with me," she confided.

Benedict hollered from below, "Katherine!"

"I have to go. I'll come back shortly to get the tray," she said and rushed off.

John's curiosity was piqued. Benedict had been in the war, he was from Pennsylvania, and he hadn't forgotten Benedict's nervous response when he'd mentioned Pruitt's name. Did Benedict know Pruitt? Had they crossed paths in Tucson due to both men being Union soldiers during the war? Everything was merely coincidental, but it made John wonder. What he needed now was time to chat with Benedict about the war. He knew that wouldn't be easy, but maybe Benedict could provide the information he needed to find Pruitt.

\*\*\*

After finding Ferguson's body, Daniels had spent the past days searching the mountains nearby for the Captain's Raiders' hideout but couldn't find anything. It was as if the Captain and his crew were ghosts that could manifest at any time, then disappear into thin air just as quick.

Besides the trouble with the Captain, Geist was stirring up trouble in town against him so much that even the mayor had paid him a visit to discuss it. He regretted listening to John. Allowing Ferguson to willfully escape was a plan that, upon reflection, had been doomed to failure.

Sitting alone in his office, Daniels pondered his next step. Rumors were circulating that Geist was leveraging the mayor to recall him and then hold a special election for sheriff. This threat wasn't new from Geist, but now with this colossal mistake of the big escape, he feared the mayor was more receptive to such an idea, with the local newspaper printing an opinion article supporting such a plan. Becoming sheriff had been a lifelong dream for Daniels, and when he'd won six years before, he'd thought he'd be in the job until he died. That had changed when Geist came to town filled with ambition to be one of the biggest landowners in the region. The two had had a cordial relationship, with Geist supporting his campaign in the last election two years prior, but that cordial relationship had come to a halt after he wouldn't enforce a court ruling against some landowners, who immediately filed an injunction and received it from

Prescott. The injunction didn't stop Geist from applying pressure on Daniels, but Daniels had acted within the law and allowed the landowners to stay. That decision started the war between both men, which now was becoming one-sided for Daniels.

Garrett burst through the door. "Sheriff, we've got trouble."

"What kind of trouble?" Daniels asked.

"Captain's Raiders," Garrett answered.

Daniels leapt to his feet and raced out the door. "Where?"

Garrett was on his heels and replied, "There's three of them, and they're tearing up Johnson's Mercantile."

Daniels took off in a sprint with Garrett following closely behind. He made the first corner, and half a block down he saw a box smash through the window and land on the street.

The townsfolk had scurried off and were taking shelter, knowing a gunfight could erupt at any time.

Daniels pulled his handgun but stopped short of going further. He turned to Garrett and asked, "Where's Wheeler?"

"Sleeping, Sheriff," Garrett answered.

"Go get him," Daniels ordered.

"But, Sheriff, there's no time," Garrett said, concerned by the order. "Don't you think we need to stop these men now?"

Several gunshots cracked inside the mercantile.

Beads of sweat ran down Daniels' temple. Normally he was calm, cool and collected, but this was rattling him.

"We, um," Daniels stuttered.

"Sheriff, are you alright?" Garrett asked.

"I'm fine."

"Sheriff Daniels, are you just going to stand there and do nothing!" Geist hollered as he strolled up, seemingly unconcerned about the Raiders down the street.

Daniels sighed. He turned to face Geist and barked, "I don't have time for your belligerence."

Geist walked up to within inches of Daniels and said, "Tsk, tsk, tsk, first you hire a Confederate, then you lose a prisoner and not just any prisoner but a Raider, and now you're standing around with your finger up your ass while other Raiders tear up old man Johnson's mercantile."

"I'm not allowing anyone to do anything. I just arrived and I'm assessing the situation," Daniels said defensively.

"Assessing? Looks more like cowardice with a dash of incompetence," Geist prodded.

Daniels had had enough. He turned back around and said, "Deputy, let's go arrest those men."

"What about Wheeler, sir?"

"No time. Let's take these men into custody, and, Garrett, if they don't listen, shoot them," Daniels said before marching off.

\*\*\*

Katherine jumped, startled by the pounding at the front door. "Oh dear, who can that be?"

"Someone clearly in need," Benedict said, shot up from the dinner table and raced to the door. He unlocked two latches and opened it to find Sheriff Daniels standing there. "Excuse me, Pastor Rawles, I apologize for coming so late."

"Oh, it's quite alright, Sheriff. What can I do for you?" Benedict said. He looked back at Katherine, who was hovering close by. He faced Daniels again and said, "Would you please come in?"

Daniels removed his hat and said, "This isn't a social call, and secondly, this matter is of some urgency."

"How can I help?" Benedict asked.

"We had an altercation at Johnson's Mercantile today; three of the Captain's men came into town and tore up the place. Deputy Garrett and I responded..." Daniels paused, his face contorting slightly before he continued. "We subdued the Raiders, but unfortunately, Garrett was shot and, well, it looks bad, real bad."

"Do you want me to come administer last rites?"

"Yes, if you could do that, I'd be much obliged."

"Of course, give me a minute to go get my things," Benedict said and hurried off.

Daniels stood in the door, looking uncomfortable.

Seeing the state Daniels was in, Katherine approached. "Sheriff Daniels, I overheard. I'm so sorry to hear about Mr. Garrett. He is such a nice man, a real gentleman."

"That he is, miss," Daniels said. He shifted the topic and asked, "Is John Smith here?"

"Right here, Sheriff," John said from the top of the

stairs.

Both Katherine and Daniels looked towards the darkened stairs but couldn't see anything.

John emerged from the shadows and slowly walked towards Daniels. "Did you kill those Raiders?"

"Yes."

"There's a good chance others will ride in, especially after they notice their men don't come back," John said.

"I'm aware of that. However, I don't anticipate them for at least a day or more," Daniels said. "Right now, I need to take care of Garrett."

"May I offer my services again?" John asked.

"I don't think that's a good idea," Daniels replied sternly.

"Sheriff, you need the manpower, at least consider it," John urged.

"No."

"I'm ready," Benedict said, entering the room to find John standing there. "What are you doing out of bed?"

"I heard the sheriff and offered my help," John answered.

Benedict raised his brow and said, "So you're coming along?"

"No, he's not," Daniels interjected.

John shook his head in frustration.

"Pastor Rawles, let's go," Daniels said, turning around and heading off into the dark of night.

Benedict exited the house and disappeared.

John made his way to the door and stared helplessly into the darkness.

Katherine came behind John and placed her right hand on his left shoulder. "You need to be in bed, resting."

"The sheriff needs me. He's just too stubborn to ask," John said and headed back to the stairs.

"Where are you going?" Katherine asked.

Without turning around, John answered, "To my room. I'm getting dressed; then I'm going to go help the sheriff." When he reappeared at the top of the stairs, his gun belt was slung over his shoulder. He found her standing at the bottom, her arms folded.

"You're still recovering," she snarled.

He walked down and stopped just in front of her. "I'll be honest, I'm still sore, but I'll be fine."

"Your ribs are still broken," she said.

"I don't need to be reminded. Every time I breathe, I can feel them," he joked.

"Sheriff Daniels can take care of himself."

He went to walk around her, but she stepped in front of him. He went to go the other way, and again, she blocked him from passing. "Please, Katherine, let me go."

"No."

"Why?"

"'Cause you're still recovering, and it's my responsibility to make sure you get better," she answered.

He looked into her eyes and asked, "Tell me why?"

She gave him a nervous look and said, "I don't know what you're implying, but it's your health and welfare that I'm most concerned about."

"Are you sure?" he flirted.

Her nostrils flared, and anger welled up inside her. "How dare you."

"Apparently I misjudged. Please forgive me," John said, fully knowing she felt something for him.

Frustrated by his accusation of her intentions, she stepped out of his way and said, "Fine, go, but if you get hurt again, don't expect me to be here to take care of you."

He stepped but stopped when he was next to her. He looked over and said, "In full disclosure, I'm going to make sure your father is fine. I'd hate for something to happen to him."

Hearing this, her anger melted away. "Thank you."

"You're welcome. I hope to be back soon with your father safe and sound," he said then exited the house to go saddle up Molly for the ride into town.

# CHAPTER EIGHT

"Honesty is the first chapter in the book of wisdom." – Thomas Jefferson

TUCSON, ARIZONA TERRITORY

JULY 23, 1876

The clock struck one. John looked at it and couldn't believe he was still at Garrett's house, waiting for Benedict to finish.

Daniels sat across the table from him but had only spoken a few words to him.

The cries of anguish from Garrett's wife and son seemed never-ending and ate away at John. Several times he had gotten up to see if Benedict needed assistance, but each time he was rebuffed.

The bedroom door finally opened and Benedict emerged, his head hung low. The cries increased with intensity, signaling that Garrett had just succumbed to his wounds. He closed the door and walked over to John and Daniels. "He's with God now."

Daniels made the sign of the cross and softly said, "May he rest in peace."

"Very sad," John said.

"Mrs. Garrett has requested a viewing at the house here and a funeral to be held in two days' time," Benedict said.

"I'll make the arrangements," Daniels said.

"No need, Sheriff, you've got issues to attend to. Don't let this distract you from that," Benedict said.

"Thank you, Pastor," Daniels said.

"It's what we do," Benedict said. He faced John. His jaw tightened and his brow furrowed. "What are you doing here?"

"I came to provide assistance," John said.

Benedict nodded.

"How about I give you a ride back to your house?" Daniels offered.

"Not necessary, I'll walk back. It's a nice warm evening," Benedict said and headed for the door.

John hopped up and followed him outside without saying goodbye to Daniels. "Can I join you?"

"It's a free country," Benedict said.

John untied Molly and walked her over to Benedict. "I haven't had the chance to thank you for once more opening your house to me. If it weren't for you and Katherine, I don't know what condition I'd be in."

"That's what good Christian people do," Benedict said.

The two men shared a few minutes of small talk until John found the courage to begin asking pointed questions about the war. "Where did you fight?"

"What do you mean?"

"During the war, where did you fight?"

"Fight?"

"Yeah, were you in Virginia, or were you out west?"

"The war? Oh no, I wasn't in the war," Benedict said.

Finding his answer odd, and needing to know, John said, "Katherine said you were in the war, that you fought."

Benedict clenched his teeth and shook his head.

Unable to see Benedict's facial expression in the dark of the night, John kept pressing. "I can understand not wanting to talk about it. Hell, I don't like to talk about it much. I find few people can relate. I just thought—"

"You thought wrong," Benedict said.

"I know you hate people like me. Hell, I don't find much to love about Yankees," John snorted.

Benedict stopped and said, "You seem well enough to move on."

"The other night when I mentioned a name, you acted strangely. Why?" John asked, ignoring Benedict's previous comment.

"I don't know what you mean," Benedict replied.

"I said the name Captain Pruitt and you practically choked. You seemed as if you'd seen a ghost."

"If you're accusing me of knowing whoever that is, you're mistaken," Benedict said and continued on his way up the street.

John caught up and asked, "I beg you, if you know who he is, please tell me."

"I don't know that name," Benedict declared.

"Are you sure? Please, I need to speak with him. It's important," John pleaded.

"Do you Southerners not know the meaning of *I don't know*?" Benedict said.

"I think you're lying," John confessed, steering the

conversation in a different direction.

"Why is this man so important to you, huh?" Benedict asked.

"Because he is," John answered.

"If you need to know some truth, I think you're the one lying. I don't believe you and this Captain Pruitt are friends. I think you want to know where this man is for other reasons," Benedict said.

"I need to find him. Why won't you help me?" John said.

"Because I don't know him, that's why," Benedict answered.

Frustrated, John stopped, mounted Molly, and just before riding off, he said, "I hope you reconsider letting me know."

"Goodnight, Mr. Smith, make sure you vacate my house by morning," Benedict ordered.

"I will," John said and rode off.

\*\*\*

The loud banging on the door woke Geist. He grumbled, stretched and hollered out, "Yeah, what is it?"

"Sorry to wake you, sir, but there's a man here who says he has critical information for you," a man replied.

"What time is it?" Geist asked, slowly rising.

"Four thirty-five, sir," the man answered.

Geist tossed the sheets off him and slipped his legs out of bed. He yawned and rubbed his eyes.

"Sir, you awake?" the man asked after getting no

reply for a minute.

"Yes, Goddamn it, I am," Geist roared. He marched to the door and threw it open. "This better be good."

The man looked scared and began to stutter, "He, ah, he said it was very important."

"Fine, fine, where the hell is he?" Geist asked.

"He's in the faro parlor," the man answered.

Geist grabbed his robe, slid his bare feet into a pair of slippers, and headed to the parlor. When he cleared the corner, he heard the distinct raspy laughter of the drunkard Jackson. Upon entering the parlor, he found Jackson tossing back a shot of whiskey. "This had better be good," Geist said, taking a seat across from Jackson.

"I came to see about getting paid and—" Jackson said.

Geist's eyes widened with anger. He leaned across the table and barked, "You woke me to get your payment?"

Seeing he needed to get to the meat of why he was really there, Jackson said, "Not exactly that. The main reason was because I linked up with the Captain. I told him what had happened to his men." Jackson hesitated and poured another drink.

Geist reached across the table and swatted the glass away. "And what did he say?"

"He, um, he's pissed. Oh boy, is he mad. I watched him take a prisoner they had and beat him to death with his bare hands."

"Did he say anything about what I offered?" Geist asked.

"Oh yeah, he had a lot to say. He said he was coming to town to exact a pound of flesh for the killing of his men, including that prisoner who escaped, and he…" Jackson said, looking down, hesitating to finish.

"Spit it out," Geist growled.

"And he said when he's done, he's coming to see you."

"He is?"

"Yes."

"And? C'mon, you imbecile, just tell me if he took the deal," Geist hollered and slammed his fist.

"Yes, he'll take the deal."

Geist eased back into the chair, a smile creased across his face.

"Can I get some payment?" Jackson asked.

"Who else knows about this?" Geist asked.

"No one, sir, I promise. I did as you told me and kept my mouth shut," Jackson said, nodding his head vigorously.

Geist looked at one of his men and nodded.

His man pulled a pistol, put it to Jackson's head, and pulled the trigger. Jackson fell out of his chair and onto the floor. His body twitched as blood slowly poured out of the large wound in his head.

Geist stood up, gave the grisly sight a brief stare and said, "Feed his body to Mr. Chang's hogs and clean up this mess. We open in a couple of hours." He stepped off and headed back to his room.

\*\*\*

Heeding Benedict's demands, John was down saddling Molly as soon as the sun rose. He deliberately slipped out of the house to avoid waking Katherine to prevent her from getting upset.

He fastened the saddlebag to Molly and inspected the contents. He then noticed he was missing his Bible. He didn't read so much as look at Elizabeth's inscriptions written throughout the book. He now remembered he'd left it in the drawer of the nightstand. "Damn," he grunted. The last thing he wanted to do was go back inside and cause a disturbance, but he couldn't leave something of such personal value behind. He bolted to the front door and slowly turned the knob. The door opened with a slight creak, but not enough to wake anyone. He slipped inside and carefully walked to the stairs and began to ascend.

When he heard a door open on the second floor, he wondered who it might be and prayed it was Benedict. The light footfalls told him it wasn't. Katherine soon appeared at the top of the stairs.

"You're up early. Still not resting, I see," she said, her hands planted firmly on her hips.

"I'm just getting something from my room," he said, clearing the top steps and passing her.

"What time did you and my father return?" she asked, following him to his room.

He quickly went into the room, found the Bible and turned around to leave. However, she stopped him when she noticed his room had been emptied of his personal things.

"Where are you going?" she asked.

"I'm well enough to move on, so I am," he replied.

"No, you're not. Just because you went out last night doesn't mean you're well enough," Katherine said sternly.

"Katherine, I'm fine. Thank you for taking care of me. It's now time for me to leave," he said.

"He's right," Benedict said from the hallway.

Katherine turned and asked, "Was this your idea?"

Before Benedict could answer, John spoke to defend him. "No, it was mine. I have things to do, and I don't have time to lie around. I came here to find someone, and I need to go do that."

Not prepared to let him leave, Katherine said, "Father, please tell him he needs to stay. We can help him find this man, this Captain Pruitt."

Benedict's face grew tight and his jaw tensed.

This was exactly what John had wanted to avoid, and now he wished he'd just left the Bible and written to have it mailed to him later.

"Mr. Smith is correct. It's time for him to leave. He and I spoke at length about this Captain Pruitt. I do not know this man."

"Are you sure, Father?" Katherine asked, hoping her father could find the compassion in his heart to help John.

"Quite sure. Now please step out of Mr. Smith's way so he may go about his business," Benedict said.

Katherine stood her ground and gave John a look of

pleading.

Right then all John wanted to do was sweep her up and hold her. It was a sensation he hadn't felt in a very long time. He could see the longing in her eyes and could literally feel her pain.

The two stood looking at each other for what felt like minutes before Benedict quickly stepped in and pulled Katherine aside. "You may go, Mr. Smith."

"Yes, of course," John said to Benedict. He looked at Katherine and said, "Goodbye."

Katherine's lower lip quivered. She was a tough and determined woman, but at this moment she was having a difficult time coping with her emotions.

John rushed past her and hurried down the stairs. He exited the house and closed the door behind him. Before he could take another step, he exhaled heavily. Not since Elizabeth had he felt so strongly for someone, and he hadn't been with a woman since her. He didn't want to leave for two reasons: one being Katherine, and the second being he knew Benedict had information but was unwilling to give it up. Just how he'd find out what that was, he'd have to figure out. After pulling himself together, he stuffed the Bible into the saddlebag, climbed onto Molly, and rode off to get a room in town.

\*\*\*

John checked himself into a hotel next to the Bella Grande, and unbeknownst to him, it was also owned by Geist. He hadn't gotten much sleep, so he planned on catching up by getting a few more hours.

He walked to the small single window of his room and was about to draw the blinds when he saw ten riders race past. By the looks of them, they were here to cause trouble. He turned and grabbed his gun belt but stopped short of putting it on. With Daniels being upset at him, he wasn't sure if his help would be welcome. He placed the gun belt on the table.

Several gunshots echoed from up the street.

He peeked out the window. The riders were out of sight, but there wasn't any doubt who had fired the shots. He grabbed his gun belt and slung it around his waist and fastened it. Daniels might not welcome his help, but he was going to need it. As he headed out the door, he grabbed his Winchester rifle and hat.

When he reached the street, more gunshots rattled in the distance. It sounded like they were at the sheriff's office. John had two choices: head there directly on foot, or go get Molly from the livery down the block. Time was of the essence, so he made out on foot. The only trouble was his ribs were not healed, and each footfall against the hardened street jolted his body and sent searing pain through him. He reached the intersection but stopped shy of crossing over. He leaned in and peeked around the corner. The riders were at the sheriff's office and had Wheeler tied up. His eyes darted around looking for Daniels, but he was nowhere to be seen. This told John that he was probably at home. With Wheeler out of the fight, this left only Daniels and him to fight ten well-armed men. John carefully looked at each rider, hoping to spot the notorious Captain, but no one seemed to fit the bill.

A man appeared from the sheriff's office, wearing a black hat with one side pinned up, adorned with a blue cord and brass device on the front.

John immediately recognized the hat as a Hardee, or what was also known as a Jeff Davis. It was widely worn by Union soldiers and officers alike. The hat told John one thing, the man wearing it must be the Captain. A rage began to build in him. It had been eleven years and now he was as close as he had ever been to the man who had killed his family. The temptation to step out and begin firing filled him, but he didn't want to just kill him, he wanted Pruitt to know who was killing him and why. How was he going to do it? How could he overwhelm nine other men to get to Pruitt? The situation was untenable, but as the past had shown him, his determination had seen him through other tough spots.

The Captain and his men had no doubt come for revenge, so they weren't going to leave until they found Daniels. This meant John had to get to Daniels and fast. He didn't look forward to the long haul across town, but it had to be done.

\*\*\*

Benedict hollered, "I'm heading to the church. I'll be back just before lunch."

Katherine replied, "Okay."

Benedict exited the house, took a deep breath and

happily looked around. Not having John there certainly added to his joy. He jumped onto his wagon and headed off.

As he entered town, he saw a man running. Upon closer look, he noticed it was John.

John spotted Benedict at the same time and called out, "Benedict, help, I need help!"

Benedict looked around, and the thought to just ignore John came to mind.

John ran up and stopped in front of his double horse drawn wagon. "Please, Sheriff Daniels needs help."

"What's wrong?"

"The Captain and his men are in town. They've taken Deputy Wheeler prisoner, and I have no doubt they're headed to Daniels' residence. I'd keep running, but my side is killing me. Please take me to his house."

Once more Benedict was involved with John, the one man he didn't want to see nor have anything to do with. But how could he say no? He liked Daniels, and if he needed help, he had to oblige. "Hop on."

John cringed in pain as he climbed onto the wagon.

Benedict cried out, "Go!" He snapped the reins and hollered again, "Go, go!"

The horse went from standing to a full run in seconds.

It took only minutes what would have taken John five times that to reach Daniels' house on the outskirts of town. Benedict pulled the reins hard when they pulled up to the front of the house. The horses came to an abrupt stop.

"Sheriff Daniels!" John hollered, jumping off the wagon. When he hit the ground, a jolt of pain shot through his body. He bent over and tried to catch his breath.

The front door of the house flew open, and Daniels appeared wearing only trousers and a pullover shirt. He was armed with a rifle in his hand. "What the hell do you want, Johnny Reb!"

"Wheeler, they have Wheeler," John gasped, his side throbbing in pain, making it hard to breathe.

"What? Who has Wheeler?" Daniels asked, a look of shock on his face.

"The Captain's Raiders," Benedict clarified.

"Where are they?" Daniels asked, pulling a suspender over his shoulder to hold his pants up.

John stood, caught his breath and replied, "The office, that's the last place I saw them, but I know they're here to get you too."

"Those sons of bitches!" Daniels said and turned to go back inside. He emerged seconds later with his gun belt around his waist and his hat on. "If those rat bastards want a fight, I'll give it to them."

"Sheriff, we're outnumbered. There's nine of them, well-armed, and the Captain is with them."

"The Captain is here too, the man himself. I saw him with my own eyes," John said.

"He is?" Daniels asked, his anger giving way ever so slightly to fear.

"It had to be him," John said.

"But you're not sure?" Daniels asked.

"Not sure, but I think it's him," John replied.

"I thought you knew the man," Benedict said, referencing John's claim of being friends with Captain Pruitt, who John suspected was the Captain.

Ignoring Benedict's snarky question, John looked to Daniels for a clear answer on what they were going to do. "We need more men. We can't fight them by ourselves."

Daniels walked to his horse and put on its saddle.

"Sheriff?" John asked.

"I'm thinking, damn it. Let me think!" Daniels growled.

"There's no time to think," Benedict said, pointing to the south.

John looked and saw a pack of riders coming their way.

"Quickly, inside the house," Daniels said.

John ran into the house with Daniels just behind him. John turned but didn't see Benedict coming; instead, Benedict took off in his wagon. "Benedict, where are you going?"

Benedict was too far away to hear and heading away from the advancing men.

"Coward left us," John spat.

"He's a man of the cloth. We can't expect him to fight," Daniels said. He gave John a warm look and nodded. "I've been an ass lately, I apologize for that."

"It's fine."

"Thank you for warning me and thank you for being here."

"Fighting is what I do," John said.

"Good man," Daniels said.

Most of the riders barreled up to the front of the house, only stopping feet from it. Several broke away and rode around the house, ensuring no one was fleeing on foot.

"That wagon went that way," a man called out from the back.

"Let them go. It wasn't the sheriff," the Captain said. He looked around the small house and ordered, "You two, go check the barn and shed. Oh, don't forget to look in the outhouse too."

Two men rode off.

"Sheriff Daniels, it's the Captain. Come on out!"

John peeked through a crack in the shutters and could see the Captain. He was a large man, with broad shoulders, and on his rugged face, a thick beard hung long and low, reminding him of Stonewall Jackson's beard.

"Sheriff Daniels, we can make this easy or hard; doesn't matter to me," the Captain said calmly. He turned and said, "Bring his deputy up here."

A man dismounted and cut the rope that connected Wheeler to a horse. They had dragged him all the way from the office.

Wheeler, cut free, didn't move. He lay motionless on the ground. His clothes were torn and covered in blood and dirt.

"He's not moving, Captain," the man said, closely examining Wheeler.

"If he won't get up, drag him over here," the Captain

ordered.

Daniels did as John did and peeked through a slit in the shutters. He cringed when he saw Wheeler's motionless body brought forward.

"Sheriff Daniels, your deputy is in bad shape, but I can attest he's not dead...yet. I'll give you a choice— come out and I won't kill him."

Daniels stood up and walked to the door.

"No, don't go out there," John urged as he grabbed Daniels' arm.

"I have to. He's my man, and if there's anything I can do to spare his life, I need to do that," Daniels said somberly as if resigned to his fate.

"They'll kill you then him. These men are butchers, I know, I know very intimately how barbaric the Captain is," John said, pleading.

"This is Tucson business. The Captain and everything else here have nothing to do with you."

"He murdered my family," John confessed.

"What? When?"

"During the war, he had my family slaughtered. Please, we must fight them. We can't give up, not now," John urged.

"I'm sorry to hear that, but none of that changes the fact that my deputy's life is hanging in the balance," Daniels declared.

"Sheriff Daniels, your deputy is running out of time," the Captain hollered.

Wheeler began to move. He barely opened his swollen eyes and mumbled something unintelligible.

"Look here, he's alive but not for long." The Captain laughed.

"Captain, you won't get away with this. No matter what you do to me, the town won't let you just come in here and kill their peace officers," Daniels yelled.

The Captain and his men began to laugh loudly.

"Sheriff Daniels, I'm here on behalf of your town. After I'm done with you, I plan on seeing a Mr. Geist to collect my payment and secure my legacy in this town. You see, Sheriff, I made a deal with the richest and most influential man in this town. So your weak threats won't steer me away from my plans."

Daniels grunted his displeasure at hearing the conspiracy. He wasn't shocked, but for Geist to go this far, he must truly want him more than gone, he wanted him dead.

"I'm going to count to three, and if you're not out here, I'm going to put a big hole in this man's head," the Captain howled.

"No, don't, Sheriff," Wheeler muttered loudly.

"You shut up, boy," the Captain snapped.

Daniels pulled away from John's grip and cleared the remaining distance to the door. He reached for the handle but stopped when John discharged his rifle through the window. He turned to see John lower the lever of his rifle and load another round.

Outside, the single round struck one of the Captain's men in the chest. The force of the bullet toppled him from the horse. He was dead before he hit the ground.

The Captain angrily barked, "Spread out and open

fire on the house!"

"What have you done?" Daniels yelled.

The Captain's men began to spread themselves out around the house and immediately began to fire upon the house. The Captain still sat in his saddle calmly. He looked at Wheeler, pulled his pistol and took aim.

Daniels threw open the door, raised his rifle and said, "No you don't!"

Before Daniels could get a round off, he was struck a half a dozen times. He dropped to his knees and fell forward dead.

"Shit," John barked. He'd been in precarious situations, but this was definitely the most serious one he'd been in, in his life. However, if he was going to go down, he would go down fighting. He took aim at the Captain and began to squeeze.

A round struck the window just above his head, causing him to duck and jerk the trigger. The rifle fired, but his aim was off. The round struck the Captain's horse.

The horse reared up and tossed the Captain off; he landed hard on the ground. Quickly he scurried to his feet and yelled, "There's another in the house. Fire, fire everything you have!"

The hail of gunfire was intense. John dropped to the floor and curled up. Glass and splintered wood flew all around him.

The barrage lasted for minutes.

"Cease fire, cease fire!" the Captain ordered.

The firing slowed then stopped.

John looked up. He was shocked that not only was he still alive, but he hadn't been hit. It was a miracle.

"Bring a torch up. Let's burn it down," the Captain ordered.

Hearing that, John knew he didn't have a chance of surviving if he remained inside. His only opportunity was now fighting it out. He got to his knees and readied himself for his final battle.

A gunshot from faraway echoed.

"Over the hill!" one of the Raiders hollered.

The Captain turned but saw nothing.

Another single crack echoed.

One of the Captain's men toppled over.

"Xavier is shot!" someone called out.

Whoever was out there provided John the diversion he needed. He got up, headed towards the back window and looked out. He spotted the man holding the lantern, took aim and fired. The round struck him in the chest. It was a clean and well-placed shot. The man dropped like a sack of beans; the lantern smashed to the ground with the oil catching the man on fire.

Another single shot cracked in the distance and once more hit one of the Captain's men.

John ran the numbers. He'd shot two men, and if this other shooter was hitting true, he'd taken out three, meaning the Captain was down to five, including himself. John spotted another of the Captain's men, took aim and fired. The round exploded from the muzzle and struck the man in the face.

"Four," John said out loud as he moved the action of

the Winchester. He saw another Raider making a run for it. He carefully aimed at the moving target and squeezed.

The man toppled to the ground dead.

"Three," John said and again moved the lever action.

The Captain cried out, "Kill them, damn it!" his voice cracking.

The distant gunfire continued when another single shot cracked, this time striking one more of the Captain's men.

John saw the man fall. "Two," John said, almost laughing. He ran to another window to try to find the last man but couldn't see him.

"Where are you going?" the Captain yelled.

John ran to the front window and caught a glimpse of a man running away. Seeing his opportunity, John stepped into the open doorway, aimed and shot the Captain in the knee.

The Captain's knee inverted and he dropped to the ground. The Captain roared in pain.

John exited the house, levered the action and squeezed; however, the hammer hit but no round fired.

The Captain heard the hammer strike and looked up to see John walking towards him. He raised his pistol and fired just as a round from the distant shooter hit him in the upper right arm. The bullet from his pistol sliced through John's shirt and skimmed his forearm. The Captain tried to cock his pistol again, but he had lost some function and strength in his arm. He fumbled with the pistol and ultimately dropped it into the dirt.

Not needing the rifle, John let it go and ripped his

Colt from his holster. He cocked the hammer, raised it and took aim. He began to apply pressure to the trigger but stopped. He didn't want to kill him like this. Thinking quickly, he ran up and pistol-whipped the Captain.

The Captain absorbed the blow and even swung himself.

John raised his arm high and came down on the top of the Captain's head. The strike was enough to cause the Captain to buckle and fall face-first into the dirt. Having the clear advantage, John hovered over him and smiled. "Do you know who I am?"

Groggy, the Captain replied, "Who gives a shit?"

John lowered the hammer on his Colt, holstered it and grabbed the Captain's shirt. He dragged him to the front porch and leaned him against the steps. "Look at me."

The Captain peered up and sneered, "Kill me if you want, just stop talking already."

"Captain Pruitt, your days of murder and mayhem have come to an end. Today you will receive the justice you've had coming to you since you murdered my family in Georgia."

"What in the hell are you talking about?" the Captain asked, his face showing shock and dismay.

The sound of a wagon came from behind John. He turned and saw Benedict riding up, a rifle in one hand, the reins in the other.

"Don't kill him. He must be tried and hung by the people of Tucson!" Benedict hollered, rearing his horses to a full stop feet from John.

126

"No! He killed my family. I'll be the one to serve justice today," John declared.

Benedict jumped out and marched over to John. "You're not thinking clearly. This man has terrorized our town for years. The people of Tucson will be the arbiters of justice."

John snatched his Colt from his holster, cocked it and pointed it at the Captain. "Captain Bartholomew Pruitt, you're guilty of the murder of my wife, Elizabeth, and my daughter, Mary. Today you'll die by my hand."

"John, stop. How do you know he's Captain Pruitt?" Benedict asked.

John let the question sink in. Benedict made a valid point. Was this man really Captain Pruitt? Remembering what West had told him back in Santa Fe, John leveled the pistol at the Captain's face and said, "Take off your jacket."

"Why?" the Captain asked.

John fired a shot; it struck the post next to the Captain's face. "Remove the jacket, then your shirt."

"Fine, I will, but I've been shot, I'll need some help," he replied.

"I'm not sure what you're doing, but I'll help," Benedict offered. He came up to the Captain and, after a few tugs, removed the thick blue jacket, then pulled off his shirt. Fresh blood poured from the wound in his upper arm.

"Move out of the way," John ordered Benedict.

"What are you looking for?" Benedict asked.

"Do you want my trousers too?" the Captain asked.

"Shut your mouth," John said as he walked over and looked at his back. When he saw his right shoulder blade, he expected to see the old brand, but it wasn't there. "It's impossible."

"What is?" Benedict asked.

"It's not him," John said, shocked. He lowered his pistol and walked off, bewildered.

Benedict walked up to John and asked, "What were you looking for?"

"It doesn't matter, it's not him," John replied.

Seeing a chance, the Captain jumped to his feet and bolted for a horse.

John calmly turned around, cocked his Colt, raised it and fired. The .45-caliber round hit the Captain in the lower back. He fell back and hit the ground.

"Don't kill him. Let the people of Tucson have their justice," Benedict argued.

John pushed Benedict back and said, "For over eleven years I searched for Captain Pruitt, but even though you're not him, you're just as bad as he is. You're an evil man, and you deserve death." John cocked the pistol again and fired. This time the round hit the Captain in the center of his back. John walked over and was now towering over him. He pushed him onto his back, cocked the pistol once more, but before he pulled the trigger, he asked, "Do you have anything to say?"

"This Captain Pruitt, it sounds like he was a good man," the Captain sneered.

Anger welled up inside John. Unable to reply, he simply pulled the trigger.

# VENGEANCE ROAD

# CHAPTER NINE

"Forgiveness is the fragrance that the violet sheds on the
heel that has crushed it."
– Mark Twain

TUCSON, ARIZONA TERRITORY

JULY 31, 1876

John rode straight for the Bella Grande after the
ceremony. He and Benedict had been honored with
medals from the mayor for bravery in their part for taking
down the Captain and his Raiders. For John, the medal,
like those he'd received during the war, was bittersweet.
He was proud of what he'd done, but the cost was high.
Out of all the bloodshed and pain, the one objective he'd
come to Tucson for seemed near impossible to fulfill.
The Captain wasn't Captain Pruitt, and not a soul in
Tucson seemed to know who he was. He was literally at a
dead end. He'd pieced everything else together and
managed to get revenge on Pruitt's detachment, but
finding the man himself now seemed impossible. He had
no leads, no one else he could think to ask except for
Benedict, and getting a word out of him was unfeasible,
especially after killing the Captain. Though he disagreed
with John's rash and fatal decision, he didn't testify
against him nor say John had done anything wrong; on
the contrary, he provided an affidavit that stated the
Captain was a risk and the killing justified. It wasn't

something John asked for, but it came as a welcome surprise.

Wheeler had recovered enough from his injuries to assume the job as sheriff. The mayor couldn't think of a better man to give the position to. Upon pinning on the badge, Wheeler asked John if he'd be a deputy. It was something he'd actually wanted, so he took the job. One of his first acts as deputy was to arrest Geist and his men and lock them up. At first Geist laughed at the arrest until he was extradited to federal authority, a decision both Wheeler and the mayor made because the only way for the legal system to work was to have Geist tried by a jury somewhere he had zero influence.

John thought about calling on Katherine but knew it was a relationship that couldn't be. Benedict would never allow it, and when John was honest with himself, he couldn't say yes to any relationship until he mentally and emotionally closed the book on finding Pruitt.

It had been a long week for him, and instead of going to his room, he went to the bar. He needed a drink, heck, he needed an entire bottle to drown out everything he'd been through over the last two weeks.

He hitched Molly to a post and sauntered inside the quiet bar. He quickly scanned the establishment. In the far back behind the bar, the bartender stood cleaning glasses with a cloth. His attire—a bow tie, white linen pressed shirt and slicked-back hair—was more formal than most bars, but it fit the atmosphere the Bella Grande was attempting to create. In between the front door and the bar lay two dozen round tables. All were empty but one. Typically at this time of day most bars would be full, but after word broke about Geist, the bar had few occupants.

At the one occupied table, four men sat, their hands full of cards and the table piled with chips, half-filled glasses and ashtrays. A large piano sat along the far left wall, and two women, scantily dressed, leaned up against it. To the far right, a wide set of stairs led to an open hallway. Along the railing, several more women stood. One looked down at John, gave him a wink and blew him a kiss.

Surprisingly, the Bella Grande didn't smell like most bars. Yes, John could pick up the aroma of cigar and pipe smoke, but the usual foul odor of stale beer or mold wasn't present. He made his way directly to the bar.

"Good afternoon, Deputy, what will it be?" the bartender asked, putting down the glass he had been cleaning and giving John his full attention.

"Whiskey," John said.

"Yes, sir," the bartender said, grabbing a bottle and glass and putting them in front of John.

John took the bottle and filled the glass. Without hesitation he tossed the shot back. He immediately poured another, but as he was going to drink it, he caught the reflection of a woman approaching him in the mirror that spanned the length of the bar. He slammed the shot and kept his eye on her.

She came up beside him and leaned on the bar. "Give me a coffee, Jack."

The bartender reached down and placed a steaming

metal cup in front of her. "There you go, Alice."

"Thank you, sweetheart," Alice said. She smelled the steam coming off the coffee but didn't take a drink at first. Out of the corner of her eye, she was staring at John.

John poured another drink but didn't shoot it right away. He looked at Alice and said, "I'm not interested."

"You talking to me?" she asked, feigning surprise.

"Is there anyone next to you?"

"Is someone having a bad day, Deputy?" she quipped.

"Have we ever talked?" John asked, trying to remember if he'd ever asked her about Pruitt.

"I don't think I've had the pleasure of speaking to you before."

"How long you been in Tucson?"

"Born and raised," she said, taking a sip.

"Ever heard of a man goes by Bartholomew Pruitt?"

She looked up and shifted her eyes around as if in deep thought. "No, never heard of him."

"Ever meet any former Union officers?"

"Is that a serious question? I've met quite a few, but none ever went by that name."

"Sorry, stupid question for a prostitute."

"Is that it?" she asked, picking up her cup.

He thought for a second then an idea popped in his head. "Do you know Pastor Rawles?"

"Deputy Smith, are you a Bible thumper come here to tell me I'm on the wrong path?" Alice snarked.

"Not at all. In fact, I don't give a shit what you do or

who you do it with, I'm merely asking if you know Pastor Rawles."

"Like know him, know him?"

Hearing her say it that way, John was curious. "Do you?"

"No, that man is wound tight as anything. I hear he hasn't had a good time in years. Some say he and his adopted daughter are…you know," Alice said just above a whisper.

"Are you referring to Katherine?"

"Does he have any other adopted daughters I'm not aware of?" She laughed. "Yes, that one with the long dark hair, the prissy one."

Growing annoyed, he moved the conversation along. "I meant do you remember when he came to town? Do you know anything about him? Besides the rumors you just mentioned, have you ever heard of any others? Do you know what unit he was with during the war, or if he used to associate with other Union officers upon his arrival?"

She cut her eyes at him and said, "Listen, Deputy, how about we go upstairs? I show you a good time and we get all these questions answered."

"Not interested."

"If you're just going to monopolize my time with silly questions, I need to go," she said.

"Do any of the other girls know Pastor Rawles?"

"What's your interest in him anyways?" Alice asked, growing suspicious.

"I'm curious," John replied.

"Then go talk to him yourself. You're a deputy and he's a pastor. I don't see why you can't just ask him," Alice said and walked off.

"Thanks for your time," John said, pulling out a silver dollar and placing it on the bar.

She heard the distinct sound, turned, picked it up and said, "Thanks." She put the coin in a small purse that hung from her wrist and walked off.

The bartender walked up and asked, "I hear you're asking about Pastor Rawles. What kind of information you looking for?"

"Do you know him?"

"I do."

"What can you tell me about him?" John asked.

The bartender didn't reply. He looked down at John's pocket and said, "A coin or two would definitely help jog my memory."

John removed another silver dollar and put it on the bar.

Jack looked at it and sneered, "I don't want one of those trade dollars. You got one of them Indian head gold dollars?"

John picked through his pocket until he found one and tossed it on the bar. "There."

Jack picked it up and took a nibble to test it. Feeling satisfied, he pocketed the coin. "Ask away."

"Do you know what unit he served in during the war?"

"I've known the pastor for many years. He's only been in here twice, but I knew him better when he visited the Gem years back. I worked there then and he'd come in. One time, like six years ago, he got rather drunk and began mumbling about the war. Said something about fighting in Georgia. That he was with General Sherman at Atlanta."

"He specifically said he was in Georgia?" John asked, his attention piqued.

"Yes, sir."

"Did he ever mention what outfit, unit he was with?"

A robust man came up to the bar and stood a few feet away. "Whiskey."

Jack gave him a quick look and said, "One moment, sir." He turned his attention back to John and said, "No, he never did, but he said something about never going home to Schenectady."

John thought hard and couldn't recall a city by that name in Pennsylvania, but that wasn't saying much for him. "Hmm, Schenectady, Pennsylvania, interesting."

"He didn't say Pennsylvania, just said Schenectady."

"Anything else, what his rank was?" John asked.

"He said something about having men—his men, to be exact. Makes me think he was an officer."

John felt warm all over, and it wasn't from the three shots. His suspicions were looking correct that there was a chance, a probable chance, Benedict might know Pruitt.

"Is that it?" Jack asked.

"One more thing, have you ever heard of or met a man named Pruitt?"

Like Alice, Jack rolled his eyes and thought. "No, sir, never."

"Nothing else you can remember?" John asked.

"Whiskey here," the man bellowed, his patience waning.

Jack stepped over, took an unopened bottle of whiskey and a fresh glass and set them in front of the man.

John sat and stewed over the few new details about Benedict he'd just learned. He didn't know how long he was sitting there, but his thoughts were broken by the man next to him.

"Hey, Deputy, sorry to disturb you, but I couldn't help but overhear you mention the city of Schenectady."

"Huh? Oh, yes, Schenectady, Pennsylvania, ever heard of the place?"

"No, I haven't."

"Me either," John said, pouring another shot.

"The reason I haven't is because Schenectady isn't in Pennsylvania, it's in New York."

John froze. Chills covered his body, and for a brief moment it felt like he was having an out-of-body experience.

"Deputy, are you alright?" the man asked, seeing John's response.

John tossed the shot back, stood up and marched out of the saloon.

\*\*\*

John had seen Benedict today, and the two had shared cordial conversation but nothing else. After the gun battle with the Captain, John had a newfound respect for Benedict. He was a man of the cloth who knew how to handle a weapon, and it had to be said that if it weren't for him, he'd be dead.

As he rode Molly towards Benedict's house, he played out the different scenarios of confronting Benedict. Some had him offering up all the information on Pruitt he'd need to find him, and others had the two men fighting. John could see why Benedict wouldn't give up Pruitt. The two must have known each other; maybe they were childhood friends and Benedict felt an obligation to protect his old friend, especially from a former Confederate. The one wild card in all of this was Katherine. Just how would she deal with him openly challenging her father and questioning his morality by harboring a man who had murdered his family? This, of course, meant he'd have to finally come clean and tell her who he really was and why he was really in Tucson.

John leapt off the horse and marched to the front door. He loudly knocked until the door opened.

"John, are you okay?" Katherine asked, wiping her wet hands on her apron, a concerned look on her face.

"Where's Benedict?" John asked, a tinge of anger in his voice.

"He's in the barn. Is something wrong?" she asked.

John pivoted and raced off the porch and headed towards the barn.

Katherine followed closely behind, peppering him with questions. "John, talk to me. What's wrong? Is someone hurt? Why won't you talk to me?"

He imagined his composure was a one-hundred-and-eighty-degree turn from the nice and gentle man she'd seen earlier today at the ceremony.

"John, what is happening?" she asked as she trotted up to him.

"I have a few questions to ask Benedict. I suggest you go back inside. You may not want to see this," John warned.

"You're scaring me. Please tell me what's going on," she groaned in fear.

Close to the barn, John called out, "Benedict, where are you?"

"I told you he was in the barn. Why are you acting like this?" Katherine asked.

Benedict emerged out of the shadows of the barn and into the warm midday sun. "Deputy Smith, what can I do for you?"

John walked up to within a foot and said, "You're not from Pennsylvania, you're from New York. Why the lies?"

Benedict smiled and said, "I could ask the same of you, Mr. Nichols."

Shocked to hear his real name mentioned, John looked stunned. He shook off the revelation and hit Benedict again with the all-important question. "Do you know Captain Pruitt? I think you do, and for some reason you're not willing to tell me."

"I've given you that answer before," Benedict replied.

"You're lying. You lied about where you were born,

you're quiet about your experiences during the war, and you've acted suspicious since the first time I mentioned that murderer's name."

"I suppose it takes a liar to know another," Benedict said.

Katherine touched John's arm and asked, "John, what is going on? What are you accusing my father of? What is my father accusing you of?"

"Katherine, let me introduce you to Corporal John Nichols of Georgia," Benedict said.

"What?"

"That's not important. What is, is that you know Captain Pruitt. I know you do, and you won't give him up."

"Is your name really John Nichols?" Katherine asked.

"Katherine, that is not important. What is important is your father knows the man who killed my wife and daughter," John replied.

"You had a wife and daughter? And they were murdered?" Katherine asked, her eyes wide with shock and dismay.

"Yes, Captain Pruitt had them murdered. He and his men came to my house. They raped my wife first and then they smashed her head in and my poor dear Mary, she was burned alive. For eleven years I've been hunting down the men who did it. I've caught up to all of them except the ringleader, Captain Pruitt. I won't rest until I find him," John said, tears of rage and sorrow filling his eyes.

Benedict looked down. He could feel John's pain, but nothing he could say could offer solace.

"Daddy, is any of this true? Do you know this Captain Pruitt? Because if you do, this man must be brought to justice," Katherine said.

Benedict shook his head.

"Please, Benedict, please find it in your heart to tell me where this man is," John pleaded.

"He's dead," Benedict blurted out.

"Dead? When?" John asked.

"Years ago," Benedict answered.

"Where is he buried?"

"That doesn't matter," Benedict said.

"It matters to me. Why didn't you just tell me? Why now?" John asked.

Benedict couldn't look John or Katherine in the eyes. He kept his stare focused on the ground.

Katherine stepped forward and took Benedict's hands. "Daddy, tell him everything so he can have closure."

"I can't," Benedict said and pulled away from Katherine. He faced away from them and kept his head down. His posture and composure were nothing like the Benedict John had met weeks ago. Gone was his strength and strong will. Something had happened to him, but what?

"How do you know he's dead?" John asked.

"'Cause I do, I can tell you that," Benedict answered.

"Is he buried in Tucson?" John followed up.

"I don't want to talk about this anymore," Benedict

said, now turning to face them again. "I won't say anything else about this. John, the man you're seeking died years ago. He's left this world. The acts he committed have been paid for."

"How do you know he's dead? What's your proof?" John asked, his tone growing insistent. Now that Benedict had finally admitted he knew Pruitt, he needed to know more, but like usual, Benedict was being resistant.

"I won't say any more about this. Captain Pruitt is dead; that is all you need to know," Benedict snapped. He glared at John and walked away.

John pursued him, with Katherine close behind. "Just tell me. Tell me where he's buried and anything else you know and I'll leave you alone, never to bother you again."

"I'm done. Now go away," Benedict growled.

"No, I won't go away. I must know. I must see his body," John pleaded, taking Benedict's arm.

Benedict jerked his arm away and yelled, "Go! There's nothing for you here! I've told you all I'm prepared to tell!" He pointed to Molly and again yelled, "GO!"

Katherine ran up and got in between the men. "Daddy, why can't you tell him these things? I don't understand. Please, just let John have peace."

"Dear daughter, I've had enough of this conversation," Benedict replied, his tone softened.

"Why can't you tell him more? This seems odd, out of place," Katherine said, her face contorted in confusion.

Benedict reached out and touched her face. "Do you

trust me?"

"Of course," she answered.

"Then trust me on this."

"Daddy, why are you hiding this information?" Katherine asked.

Once more he found it hard to look into her eyes.

"Was this Captain Pruitt a friend? Is there something more to this?" Katherine asked in a pleading tone.

Benedict shook his head.

"Please, Daddy, just tell him. You'd want to know too. If something happened to me, wouldn't you ride until the ends of the earth finding answers? I know you would. I know you'd never give up getting justice for me."

Still shaking his head, Benedict mumbled, "Please just stop."

"Stop why? Daddy, what are you hiding?"

"I can't say any more about Pruitt because whatever I say will rip this family apart and break your heart," Benedict said, tears welling in his eyes.

Katherine was speechless hearing those words; however, John wasn't and chimed in, "Benedict, please let me know everything you know so I may end this chapter in my life. I've spent the past eleven years searching and I'm so close. Just please give me this one thing."

"Daddy, please tell him."

"I can't, because—"

Cutting him off, Katherine asked, "Because why?"

"You'll never look at me the same way. You'll never forgive me," Benedict confessed.

"Forgive you? Daddy, now you're scaring me," Katherine said.

John put his hand on the back strap of his Colt and asked, "Benedict, answer this one question. Were you there?"

Benedict saw John's hand positioned on his pistol. He could feel that this was escalating to a point of no return and that they'd already gone past the tipping point. He did know all the answers to John's questions, but to express them would forever alter his life with Katherine. For so long he'd been living with guilt. He'd hidden it well, but the gun battle with the Captain, the smell of gunpowder and the sight of blood had jolted the memories of his experiences in the war front and center. Maybe it was God's will that John had come to town and upon his arrival saved Katherine like he had. Was this all destiny? Their meeting wasn't chance. Was God finally giving him the opportunity to admit his guilt? There are times in life when the past collides with the present, and this was one of those times. He looked John in the eyes and calmly said, "Yes."

Instinctually, John pulled his Colt and cocked the hammer. He leveled it at Benedict and snapped, "You were there? You saw my family murdered?"

"I was there, but I did not see your family murdered. I was at the estate," Benedict confessed.

John stepped forward.

Katherine turned and faced John, putting herself in between the men. "Lower the gun."

"He was there, Katherine," he said to her. Facing

Benedict, he asked, "How come I never heard about you, huh?"

"It's complicated," Benedict answered.

"John, lower the gun. Let us talk about this calmly. Daddy is finally admitting what he knows. This is what you wanted. Now put the gun down," Katherine said.

"Get out of the way, Katherine," John warned.

"And if I don't, are you prepared to shoot me?" she asked.

John stepped to the side; Katherine followed, always keeping herself in between Benedict and the muzzle of the pistol.

"Move," John said.

"No, you'll have to kill me."

"Damn it, Katherine, move!" John barked.

"John, you came here looking for answers. You're not going to get them pointing a gun at my father," she said.

"He's not really your father. He's a man that found you. He came out here to escape his past and happened upon you, nothing more," John said.

"That sounds familiar. Listen to yourself, who else has done that? You!" Katherine said.

"It's not the same," John said.

"Is it not in some ways? War is ugly, brutal; horrible things happen," Katherine said.

"I never murdered women and children," John said.

"Neither did I," Benedict said.

"Yes, you did. You just admitted you were there," John said, shifting to the right to put his sights on

Benedict, but Katherine shifted too.

"John, put down the gun," Katherine said, this time walking up to him and standing right in front of the muzzle.

Feeling uncomfortable with her so close to the weapon, he lowered it.

She put her hand on it and pushed it down farther. "Hear him out, please."

"I was there, meaning I was at the plantation estate. We were spread out across the area. Several of my men went to adjacent farmhouses. That was where a few encountered your wife and daughter. Their orders were not to kill or rape, but to take what wares, food, and supplies the army needed. Sherman was moving through Georgia at such a pace the supply train was over a week or more behind. In order for us to keep advancing at that rate, we needed to pillage the countryside. No orders were ever given to murder, but situations could get heated and things could get out of control. What happened that day was regrettable. I've lived with it for a long time."

"You're talking as if you were the commanding officer. You said *my men*. If you didn't give the order to murder my family, then Captain Pruitt did," John said.

"No, he didn't."

"He did. I interrogated others, and they said he was the officer who gave the orders. No one ever mentioned you, so it had to be him."

"He didn't. I know for a fact he never gave an order to murder," Benedict said.

"How can you say that?" John asked.

"Because I'm Captain Pruitt," Benedict confessed.

Katherine turned ashen.

John pushed Katherine out of the way, raised the pistol and advanced towards Benedict.

Benedict didn't flee. He raised his arms to the sky and began to pray. "Lord God, forgive me for the sins I have committed and forgive this man for the acts he's about to commit. He does not understand that the path to heaven lies in forgiveness. Fill this man's heart with grace, oh Lord."

John stopped a foot from Benedict and placed the muzzle of the Colt against his forehead. "Get on your knees."

Katherine ran at John, but he pushed her down. "Don't get in my way, Katherine."

Benedict dropped to his knees but continued praying. "Oh Lord, please take me into your arms. Let me leave these chains of mortal life and be with you in heaven."

"Stop praying and look at me," John said.

Katherine jumped to her feet and again ran at John.

Once more he shoved her away. "Open your eyes and look at me. I want you to see the man who is about to kill you."

Benedict did as John said, "Forgive me, oh Lord."

John began to apply pressure to the trigger.

Katherine got up again, but this time she didn't run at John. She pulled the small knife she carried in her boot and put it to her own throat. "If you kill my father, I'll end my life too. I will slide this blade across my throat."

John heard her threat but didn't quite believe it; however, he did stop applying pressure to the trigger.

Benedict kept praying.

"By killing my father, you're killing me too," Katherine said.

Unable to focus, John glanced at her. She was on her knees, holding the small knife to her neck so hard the sharp edge had slightly cut the flesh. A thin stream of blood was running down past her collar. "Put the knife down," John ordered.

"No, I won't. I will take my life if you take his. I swear," she said and pressed harder, causing the blade to cut deeper.

"Katherine, put down the knife," John again warned.

"I never knew the man you've mentioned, nor have you ever met him. I've only known him, the man who risked his own life to save mine. The man who turned to God, who built me a home, who raised me, who loved me. He taught me good Christian values, read me stories at night, taught me how to cook, and let me be me. I wouldn't know life without him, and if you're going to snatch him away from me, I'll go with him."

"Daughter, don't. This is meant to be. This is clearly God's will," Benedict said to her.

"No, Daddy, I won't let him murder you. I don't know what happened that day, but I do believe what you say. I've read enough about war to know that sometimes men commit evil and that sometimes good men do bad things. I don't think you are either. I believe you, I believe you were there but that a few men did evil things that you couldn't control."

"I did do wrong. I covered up their crimes. I didn't report them. I let their evildoing go unchecked, and for that I committed a sin against God and mankind," Benedict said.

"You see, he admits it," John said. His temper flared again. He looked back at Benedict and asked, "Are you ready to die?"

"I'll do it, John. Believe me, I will. You'll be murdering both of us, and that will make you no better than the evil men who DID murder your wife!"

John looked at her again and saw the blood was streaming down heavier, telling him she had the knife pressed firmly into her skin. "Put down the knife."

"No."

"Katherine, it's my time," Benedict said.

"Then it's mine too," she said.

John could see the determination in her eyes. If she did go through with it, his actions would cause her death, even though his hands weren't on the blade. Frustrated, he lowered the pistol, de-cocked it and holstered it.

Katherine ran to Benedict and fell into his arms. "Oh, Daddy."

"Don't cry, sweet daughter."

"Why didn't you ever tell me?"

"My sins are mine to bear, not yours. Will you forgive me?"

"Yes, yes, I will."

John walked off. He'd found the man he'd sought for so long, but the cost of bringing justice was too great.

Unable to even look at Katherine or Benedict, he went to Molly and rode back to town.

# CHAPTER TEN

"The education of a man is never completed until he
dies."
– Robert E. Lee

TUCSON, ARIZONA TERRITORY

AUGUST 7, 1876

When word reached Katherine that John was planning on leaving, she sent him a letter and requested he visit her before he departed.

John let days pass before he replied, informing her he'd honor her wish but with one condition, that Benedict not be there.

She agreed and the two set a date and time.

John rode up to the front of the house and tied Molly to the hitching post near the porch. As he got off her, a tinge of pain shot through him. His ribs were still healing, and even the subtlest of movements would sting.

Katherine watched him through the large front window and immediately came out when she saw him favor his side. "You know you shouldn't be traveling. You need more rest."

He looked up at her and said, "They're much better, really."

The two stood, neither moving nor saying a word. They hadn't seen nor talked to each other except for the letters since that day. An uncomfortable energy hung over the reunion.

Finally breaking the silence, Katherine asked, "Do you want some tea or coffee?" Her hands clasped tightly together.

"Ahh, no, thank you, I had my fill of coffee at the Bella Grande," he replied.

"I…" she said but stopped short of finishing her thought.

He took a step forward and said, "Thank you for your letter. I'll admit that had you not written, I would have just left, and now that I'm here, I know that would have been a mistake I'd regret."

She too took a step forward and was now at the top of the steps. "It's good to see you. I didn't know if you'd even reply. In fact, I imagined you ripping the letter up."

A warm breeze swept in from the south.

He removed his hat and said, "It's a beautiful morning. Maybe we can go for a walk." He then looked past her and into the house.

Noticing his glare, Katherine said, "He's not here. He had business at the church."

"How about that walk?" he said.

"Of course," she replied, walking down the steps.

He lifted his right arm slightly and she took it. Like a gentleman, he escorted her across the front yard towards an expansive lot that overlooked the mountains to the west.

The two carried on with small talk, both deliberately ignoring the one thing that both of them couldn't stop thinking about.

John came to a stop and turned to face Katherine. He opened his mouth, but all the words he had rehearsed couldn't come out.

She took his hands and squeezed tenderly. "Let me speak first."

"Um, no, I want to say something," he replied.

"No, please," she said and lowered her gaze to the ground to gather her thoughts. Once she'd found the words, she looked into his eyes and said, "There's so much I've been wanting to say to you since that awful day. The first was to apologize. I can't imagine how hard your life has been since you first found your family murdered. The pain you must have been dealing with all of these years must have been incredible. Discovering my father was there was beyond shocking." She cleared her throat and continued, "I wanted to tell you and I hope you hear me...I believe him, I don't think he was responsible. War is horrible, and yes, I know I never experienced it, but I've seen firsthand just how evil men can be. I'll finish by saying that I'm sorry, deeply sorry for what happened to you and for the role you think my father might have played in it."

Since that day, John had spent countless minutes going over the events and had come to accept how it ended. He understood that she'd defend Benedict, and for him, he knew he'd never truly know what happened, but if killing him meant her life would end, he couldn't have that on his conscience.

Seeing his silence, she asked, "How are you?"

"I'm fine," he answered.

"I hear you're leaving," she said.

John looked over her shoulder towards the mountains. He knew she'd ask, but for some reason hearing the words from her hit him harder than he imagined.

"John, is everything alright?"

Finally looking at her, he replied, "To be honest, it's not. It's odd for me to say this, but I'm heartbroken. I wanted to find another word to use, but I can't. That's exactly what I am. You see, Katherine, I kinda fell for you, I know it's not fair to say that, but I did. I even had thoughts about you and I, and then...then the situation with Benedict, or whatever his name is, happened. There's no way you and I could ever be, and that's assuming you felt like I did."

"Oh, John," she said, stepping closer to him.

"I've never felt like this for another woman since Elizabeth, and it tears me up that you and I will never be able to explore that potential love."

"Could we try?" she urged, taking his hand.

With his other hand, he touched her cheek. "No. Even though I have closure with your father, seeing him would only bring everything up. I'm sorry, but I have to go. I need to leave Tucson."

"Where will you go?" she asked.

John looked around in all directions and answered, "I hear the Pacific Ocean is a sight to see. Then again, I've heard they need lawmen in the Midwest, places like Dodge City and Deadwood; or maybe I'll head north, go see the Great Salt Lake."

"Why not go back to Georgia?"

"There's nothing there for me now; plus I like it out west, I do, I really do. Will you finally go to Prescott?"

"Yes, Father and I are discussing it now."

"Good, I'm so happy to hear that," he said and smiled. "Katherine, you're a gem, a real one-of-a-kind woman. You have the biggest heart and strongest will. Whatever man convinces you to take his hand will be blessed, truly blessed."

She blushed. "Oh hush, I don't even want to think about men—other men, that is—right now."

Unable to control himself, John leaned in and kissed her on the cheek. He held his face close to hers for a moment and pulled back. "Thank you."

"For what?"

"For opening my heart again. I'll be eternally grateful."

Tears formed in her eyes. "Oh, you flatter me too much."

"It's one thing us Southern men are known for," John said with a wink.

She returned his kiss with one of her own, but this time kissed his lips. When she pulled back, she touched his face and said, "Father will be home soon."

"Then it's best I be going."

She wiped a couple of tears that had broken free from her eyes and said, "Will you write me? Can you do that? I don't want to lose contact with you."

"Of course," he said.

The two walked back to Molly.

She gave him an embrace and once more kissed him. "Goodbye, John Nichols."

John tipped his hat and said, "Goodbye, Ms. Katherine, I hope we cross paths again." He leapt onto Molly, wrenched her reins to the right, and trotted away.

Katherine watched John ride until he was out of sight.

## THREE MILES NORTH OF TUCSON, ARIZONA TERRITORY

John slowed Molly until she came to a full stop. Ahead of him the trail split; the western trail meandered through a rocky outcropping and disappeared. Facing him, the northern trail slowly winded through the wide valley floor, and to his right, the eastern trail cut across the rolling hills and vanished over a small hilltop. He sat and thought which direction sounded the best. He patted Molly's neck and said, "Where should we go, girl?"

He knew of the opportunities in California, but he wasn't a businessman and would more than likely only find work being a laborer. Salt Lake sounded interesting to see, but what then? He wasn't a Mormon, so what exactly would he do there? The idea of the Midwest sounded intriguing, and from his travels he'd heard they always needed lawmen. It was true he wasn't trained in law enforcement, but what he did know was many lawmen in the west of the Mississippi were merely outlaws who changed sides and wore a badge. There was that old saying, 'Sometimes it takes an outlaw to catch an outlaw.'

John patted Molly again and said, "Well, girl, I think I've made up my mind. Let's go to Dodge City."

# EPILOGUE

"Associate with men of good quality if you esteem your own reputation; for it is better to be alone than in bad company." – George Washington

## DODGE CITY, KANSAS

## AUGUST 20, 1876

John was happy to have finally arrived at the outskirts of Dodge City. He'd heard so much about it, so his expectations were riding high. As he and Molly slowly trotted into the city limits, the first thing he took notice of was the sign.

*The carrying of firearms is strictly prohibited.*

He stopped and stared at the sign. This wasn't the first time he'd seen a sign like this. It wasn't entirely uncommon to have the municipal leaders try to control the numbers of guns on their streets. However, the reputation of Dodge City preceded it, so the sight of the sign told him whoever was in charge was attempting to clamp down on the rowdiness Dodge had become synonymous for. "It being our first day in Dodge, we best abide by the rules," he said as he scratched Molly's neck. "I suppose we need to deposit the irons at the sheriff's office," he said out loud. Seeing a man walk by, John called out, "Where's the sheriff's office?"

The man stopped and pointed. "Down around the corner."

John tipped his hat and said, "Thank you." He rode to the office and hopped off Molly. He stretched and looked around.

A tall man stepped out of a door marked Dodge City Police. He wore a white shirt tucked into black slacks and a long thick black overcoat. His face was rugged with a thick long mustache. He covered his head with a wide-brimmed hat and gave John a careful look over. "Can I help you?"

"I saw the sign about firearms. Do you want me to check them with you?" John asked.

"See my brother inside," the man said and walked off.

John pulled his rifle and headed into the office.

Inside, he found a single man sitting behind a large desk, his feet on top of it and his head in the newspaper. "What can I do for ya?" the man asked, not looking away from his paper.

"I'm here to check my firearms," John said.

The man lowered the paper and gave John a look. "Where ya from?"

Not wanting to lie, John spit out, "Georgia."

"What's your business in town? Cattle?" the man asked.

"No, I'm looking for work as a lawman," John confessed.

"Are you now? What's your name?" the man asked, smoothing out a similar mustache to the man he'd met just outside.

"Name is John, John Nichols."

"Well, John Nichols, I'm Assistant Marshal Wyatt Earp, and I don't believe Marshal Deger is looking for deputies."

John walked up and stuck out his hand. "Nice to meet you, Assistant Marshal Earp."

Earp looked at John's hand and slowly offered his. "Nice to meet you, Mr. Nichols. Now put your guns down on the table; I'll get them checked in. Make sure when you leave town you get them."

"I will, don't you worry," John said, doing as Earp ordered.

Earp went back to his newspaper.

"When can I talk with Marshal Deger?" John asked.

"He'll be back later. I suggest you come back tomorrow though."

"Sounds good, thank you," John said and headed for the door.

"Say, Nichols," Earp called out.

"Yes," John replied.

"You're wasting your time here. If you're looking for opportunity, I'd suggest you head to Deadwood. Men are becoming rich overnight there."

"Is that right?" John asked, noting he'd heard this before.

"Yes, my brother Morgan and I are leaving for there in a couple of weeks."

"Then it appears there will be an opening here," John acknowledged.

"You don't want to work for Marshal Deger. He's...how do I put it, too obliging to hooligans and rowdy cowboys."

"I'll keep that in mind," John said, feeling optimistic that he just might have a chance now to get hired.

"Be smart, go to Deadwood," Earp said before lifting the paper again.

"I'll keep that in mind," John said and exited the office. The street in front of him was bustling with activity. If Deadwood offered greater opportunity, what must those streets look like? he thought. Pushing the idea out of his head, he decided he would take advantage of the energy and excitement of Dodge City. He stepped off the walkway and looked down the street. His eyes followed along the street frontage until it settled on a sign that read *BAR*. A drink sounded good and he had something to celebrate. A broad smile stretched across his face because for the first time in a long time, he was in a town to experience life, not take it.

THE END

READ AN EXCERPT FROM G. MICHAEL HOPF'S
BEST-SELLING POST-APOCALYPTIC BOOK
**THE END**
**BOOK ONE: THE NEW WORLD SERIES**

October 15, 2066

## Olympia, Washington, Republic of Cascadia

Haley stood, staring through the thin pane of glass that separated the chilly sea air of the Puget Sound and the warmth of her living room. She looked at the capitol building in the distance. Its sandstone dome towered over the other buildings in the city, as it had for the past 138 years. At one time, it was the capitol of a single state; now it was the capitol of her country, a country born out of chaos and destruction.

She tore her gaze away from the distance and looked down at the photo she held in her hand. She touched the faces of the family depicted. Tears began to well up in her eyes as she passed her fingers across the photo. It contained four smiling faces; a portrait of a once-happy family, her family. More tears came as she thought back to the day the picture was taken. She remembered it vividly, as though it was that very morning. Haley closed her eyes and pressed the photo against her chest; the tears ran down her cheeks and hung from her chin. She remembered her father holding her tight as she sat on his knee; he kissed her many times on her head and told her how proud he was that she had tied her own shoes that day. She longed for that innocent time when she had no concerns or cares. She longed for the days when her family was together and happy. Not long after that photo was taken, her innocent world collided with the harsh realities of mass murder and apocalypse. Her family was to be ripped apart by this new reality, and what remained would never be the same.

A knock at her front door jolted her back to present. She quickly wiped the tears from her face and placed the photo in the pocket of her sweater. She walked toward the front door, but before she opened it, she turned to the mirror that hung on the wall in the foyer and looked at herself. She made sure she had wiped all the tears away and fixed her graying hair.

"You can do this, Haley," she said, attempting to reassure herself of the difficult task she had before her.

She turned and opened the door. On the porch before her were three people. The first was a man in his thirties, John, the lead reporter for the *Cascadian Times*. He was accompanied by two photographers, neither of whom could be more than twenty-five years old. They were all postwar babies; none of them knew the horror and brutality of the Great Civil War.

"Mrs. Rutledge?" John asked as he reached his hand out.

"Yes, please call me Haley." She grasped his hand firmly and shook.

She greeted the other two and invited everyone into her house. They shared small talk as the photographers set up equipment for the photo shoot that would follow the interview.

"Mrs. Rutledge, when you're ready to begin, let me know," John said.

"John, please, call me Haley."

"Yes ma'am," he answered with a sheepish grin.

Haley sat nervously, her hands rigidly clasped on her lap. She rubbed her fingers in anticipation of the first question.

"Haley, first let me thank you for letting us into your home. It is an honor to be able to speak with you and to get your personal story and perspective."

"You're very welcome, John. I have to admit, I'm a bit nervous. As you know, I don't like the limelight nor have I ever been one for doing interviews. If it weren't for your family connection you wouldn't be here. I knew your father; he was a friend and colleague to my own father. It was only when I heard you would be the one conducting this interview that I agreed," Haley said. She sat very straight and looked at John directly.

"I do know that our families have had some connection in the past and, again, thank you. Let me then get right into this."

Haley just nodded her approval.

"Next week marks the fiftieth anniversary of the Treaty of Salt Lake. It was that treaty that gave our young republic the formal victory over our opponents and gave birth to our country. Your father was in Salt Lake for that signing. What can you tell me about him?"

Haley chuckled a bit before she answered. "Wow, that is quite the question. What can I tell you about my father?

Where do I begin?" She paused for a moment before she continued, "Are you asking me about how he was then?"

"I can see how that can be a vague question, I'm sorry. Let me start again. Your father was very instrumental in the founding of this country; he is one of our founding fathers, as some would say. While many praise him for his sacrifice, there are some now that question some of his actions during the Great Civil War. How would you describe him?"

"I have heard some of those revisionists who now, in the protection of our hard-fought freedom, question the means by which it was gained. To them I say, 'you didn't live it, you were not there.' It is easy to sit in the comfort of liberty handed to you, swaddled in the bloodied cloth of our revolution," Haley said firmly. "If you are here to question my father's actions, then I feel we should start with who my father was and where he came from. The man I knew was a loving and protective man. He cared for me and the rest of his family and was willing to do whatever it took to ensure our survival. Many look back on history without looking at context. You have to have lived it to truly understand why anyone did what they did. My father was a pragmatic man who took direct action when it benefitted those whom he pledged to protect. He was not always a pragmatist, though." Haley paused; she shifted in her seat and then continued with a softer tone in her voice. "Daddy was very open about his life. He told me stories from his past. Many times, he told me that life will show up and change the way you look at the world; that there would be incidents that would shake you to the core and shift your way of thinking. My daddy had a few of those moments, the first one I can remember him telling me happened back when he was a Marine in Iraq. What happened there changed him as a person and set him on the course that would lead us to this living room today. I hope you planned on being here a while, because I am going to set the record straight."

Get **THE END** wherever fine books are sold

READ AN EXCERPT FROM G. MICHAEL HOPF'S
Best-Selling Thriller
## DAY OF RECKONING

## PROLOGUE

South Atlantic

January 14, 2000

Barrett Schumarr stared through the thick glass that separated him from test subject three eighteen.

Three eighteen squirmed, but the restraints held him tightly to the chair.

Schumarr glanced at his pocket watch with anticipation that soon the minor squirms would evolve into violent spasms. If three eighteen was like the previous test subjects, the spasms would be closely followed by death.

The room rolled to the left.

"The storm is getting closer," Charles said, referring to the ship's dramatic rolling and pitching caused from the building waves.

Charles was Schumarr's assistant and often a harsh critic and skeptic of his.

Schumarr paid no attention. His gaze darted between his watch and the man.

Three eighteen quit squirming.

"He's stop moving. Make a note on the time," Schumarr ordered.

Charles did as he was commanded and jotted down

notes on a clipboard.

Schumarr exited the observation room and started towards three eighteen but stopped when the man's head quickly lifted.

"Can you hear me?" Schumarr asked.

Three eighteen opened his eyes and looked in Schumarr's direction.

Schumarr could see he wasn't looking at him, he was looking *through* him. "Can you hear me?" Schumarr asked again as he snapped his fingers loudly near three eighteen's ears.

Three eighteen jerked his head. Thick drool dripped from his lips and sweat streamed down his stubbled face.

"Make a note that three eighteen is nonresponsive to my commands. He appears to be lucid, but he's displaying some sort of catatonic state. This is a different response than before. This is interesting, very interesting," Schumarr said looking at his watch. "We've past the time of when the other subjects began violently thrashing."

Charles feverishly wrote.

Schumarr bent over and looked closer in his eyes. "His pupils are dilated, fully."

Three eighteen continued to stare ahead.

"Hello, are you there?" Schumarr said and clapped his hands inches from three eighteen's face.

This time he locked eyes with Schumarr.

"There you are," Schumarr said with a broad smile.

Three eighteen furrowed his brow as a look of anger grew on his face.

Schumarr cocked his head and asked, "Tell me what

you're feeling?"

Three eighteen matched Schumarr's gesture by also cocking his head.

"Tell me, how do you feel?"

No response.

Three eighteen's eyes rolled back into his head and his body tensed.

Schumarr wondered if this was the beginning of the end. *Is he about to spasm then stroke out like all the others before him?* Schumarr looked over his shoulder to see Charles staring. "Don't gawk, write! Write everything you're seeing here!"

"But we're filming too!" Charles fired back.

"Write, damn it. Put down everything you're seeing in the moment. It's important! And don't argue with me."

Charles went back to scribbling quickly.

A loud snap caught Schumarr's attention. He turned to find three eighteen had broken the leather strap holding his right arm. With his right arm free, he reached across and undid his left.

Schumarr stepped forward to stop him but was pushed back hard. He stumbled backwards and fell, hitting his head against the bulkhead.

Charles looked on in horror as the leg restraints were the next thing he undid.

"Stop him!" Schumarr barked.

Charles came into the room but froze when he saw three eighteen stand and turn to face him.

A look of pure anger was etched on three eighteen's face. He stepped away from the chair and stared at

Charles. Thick drool spilled from his gaping mouth and ran down his shirt.

Charles tried to flee but wasn't fast enough.

Three eighteen caught him at the door and dragged him to the floor.

Schumarr watched in fascination as Charles was beaten mercilessly.

Charles tried to fight back but the onslaught was too much.

Three eighteen pinned a wailing Charles down by holding his shattered arms to the floor. He opened his mouth and spit a large amount of saliva into Charles' face much of which went into his mouth.

Charles gagged and threw up.

Displaying incredible strength, three eighteen reached down with his right hand and ripped Charles' jaw off and tossed it aside.

Blood poured from Charles' now gaping face. He gasped a few times then died.

With Charles dead, three eighteen turned his attention to Schumarr who had crawled to the far corner of the room.

Schumarr's eyes widened with an odd joy. Deep down he was happy; it appeared he had finally succeeded at creating something unique and equally terrible.

The door burst open. Two armed men raced in.

Three eighteen turned towards them.

They raised their rifles, but just before they could open fire, Schumarr yelled, "Don't kill him. I need him alive!"

With vicious intent, three eighteen charged the guards but only made it to within arm's reach before being hit in the head with the butt of a rifle. He fell to his knees, grunted and lunged again. A second hit to his left temple knocked him out. He fell to the floor unconscious.

Schumarr stood, wiped his hands on his white lab coat and said, "Outstanding!"

The guards gave Schumarr a perplexed look.

Unsure of how long he'd be out, Schumarr ordered, "Take him back to his cell."

They slung their rifles and scooped up three eighteen's limp body.

"And triple restrain him," Schumarr barked.

"Yes, sir," one replied.

"And make sure you wash. Toss, better yet, burn those clothes," Schumarr warned.

The men looked at their clothing, each other and back to Schumarr. They nodded and exited, three eighteen's bare feet dragging across the blood-covered floor, leaving a trail out the door.

Franz, Schumarr's senior assistant, stepped into the room carefully avoiding the gathering pools of dark red blood and not giving a care for his fellow assistant's death and said, "Dr. Schumarr, Mr. Clayton has requested to see you immediately."

"See?"

"Yes, he's here. He just landed."

The ship shook and heaved again.

Franz cringed and gave Schumarr a distressed look.

Schumarr stepped over Charles' dead body and patted Franz on the shoulder. "Don't be concerned. This ship was made for such storms."

Franz replied with a sheepish smile.

"I'm glad he wants to see me because I want to see him."

"What do I do with Charles' body?" Franz asked.

"Take it to examination room four," Schumarr said as he exited. He paused, turned around and looked at Charles' body. "And make sure you confirm he's dead. If he's not, restrain him too. I'll be back down later to conduct an autopsy."

"Shut down?" Schumarr howled.

"Dr. Schumarr, our benefactors have pulled their funding. We're out of money."

"But I've finally made significant progress with Project Sleeper," Schumarr exclaimed.

Clayton shook his head. He didn't come to debate, he came to ensure the project was shut down.

"Don't you see? We've been searching for the perfect formula, the perfect combination to make the perfect bioweapon and I'm very close."

"That's a lot of *perfects*," Clayton mocked.

"I just need more time."

"You've had plenty of time," Clayton said.

"We're close. I just need more time. These sorts of things don't happen overnight!" Schumarr snapped.

"Dr. Schumarr, enough, you've had five years. They're cutting us off. It's over!" Clayton yelled, his nostrils flared with anger.

"It's not over! Find money somewhere else."

"I know your brown-skinned friend, Yasser, loved this project. He blinded his father with the vision of creating the one, and I'll use your word, perfect solution. But it's cost us five years and half a billion dollars. While you fiddled away years experimenting, precious financial resources that could have gone to financing real attacks were squandered. Enough of the games, I'm tired of it. We're fighting a war against the imperialism of the United States. It's a real war, a war fought with real weapons, not weapons only found in science fiction."

Schumarr's spine tensed. He stood tall, clenched his square jaw and slowly ground his teeth. Anger began to well up inside him.

Seeing a change in his composure, Clayton shifted his tone and said, "Doctor, we all appreciate your efforts, it's just too late now, I'm sorry. Our alliance with your friends, the sheepherders, hasn't been this fragile, we need to preserve what we can. We must go back to more conventional means if we're to see our vision of a one world socialist order established. Our efforts need to be refocused on taking control of one of their political parties and from there we can destroy America from the inside out."

Schumarr didn't reply. He narrowed his eyes and stared past Clayton out the window to the high waves cresting on the rolling ocean.

"Go pack your personal belongings," Clayton ordered.

"Give me at least another week," Schumarr pleaded.

"We don't have another week. I have helicopters picking us up tomorrow once we clear the storm."

"You go, leave me, I need to finish this, please," Schumarr begged, his hands clasped as if he were praying.

"I can't leave you. We're scuttling the ship tomorrow. Charges are being set now. We can't leave any evidence," Clayton said. He hung his head and began to feel sympathy for Schumarr. He too had been convinced about the project in the early days, but lost faith when the years dragged on with no results. "I'm sorry, Barrett."

"This was your idea, wasn't it?" Schumarr asked.

"Honestly, yes. I'm done," he answered and paused. He took a step towards Schumarr and said, "I should tell you before you hear it once we make landfall tomorrow."

"What?"

"Project Titan," Clayton said.

Schumarr shook his head and grumbled something unintelligible under his breath.

"What did you say?" Clayton asked.

"How do you know about that?"

"Someone on your team has a big mouth."

"Who?"

"So it's true?" Clayton asked.

Schumarr lowered his head and shoulders. He sat down on the chair next to him and sighed.

"What were you thinking?" Clayton asked.

"I'm a scientist. We never throw out findings. You never know where they might lead you. New discoveries, rewriting history," Schumarr mumbled.

"Christ, if that thing gets out, it will kill us all. Are you crazy?"

"I was merely exploring a different angle. I meant to discuss this with everyone later."

"Well, your assistant Charles thought it best we all know *now*. I'm sorry, Barrett, I really am, but you've turned this into nothing more than a shit show. You were tasked with creating a lethal virus that would cripple America; instead you turned your attention to making monsters."

"I'm sorry, I was just going where the science led me."

"Where is it?" Clayton asked.

"Down below. He's secure, I swear," Schumarr said, looking up with weary eyes.

"He's secure? What does that mean?" Clayton asked, his tone showing concern.

"Today we had a breakthrough. It was marvelous. Project Titan took a big step today."

"Destroy Project Titan, Project Sleeper, all of it!"

"No, please, I have years' worth of data, findings. They might reconsider."

"It's not your work, they own it, they paid for it. No, it must all be destroyed."

"Why? Please!"

Tired of the debate, Clayton walked to the door of his stateroom, opened it and simply said, "Be ready to leave tomorrow."

## January 15, 2000

"Yasser, listen to me. We cannot let this end now. Go tell your father, please," Schumarr begged. His hand gripped the phone receiver tightly.

*"Dr. Schumarr… Barrett, I'm sorry, my father made up his mind. We are moving in a different direction now."*

"At least let me save all my findings, my logs."

*"My father gave specific instructions to have it all destroyed."*

"Why? It doesn't make any sense. Why have me even work on this only to destroy it all when we're so close?"

Yasser paused.

"Are you there?" Schumarr asked.

*"Yes."*

"At least tell me why."

*"Barrett, we know about the other thing you were working on. We didn't fund you so you could create something none of us have control over. You see, my father likes control and this, this he can't be. We have no assurances that once this gets out it won't destroy us too."*

"I'll get rid of it, I promise, but keep Sleeper alive, please."

*"I'm sorry but no. We're focused on more conventional means to strike at the United States and its allies. Ones that use commercial airliners."*

"Jets, commercial jets? No one hijacks anymore."

*"It's more than that, you'll see. We hope to execute that plan sometime in late 2001."*

Schumarr shook his head wildly and said, "Yasser, I've known you for how long? Six years, seven. You know

I can do this."

*"Barrett, I consider you a friend, but I'm sorry, my father is no longer interested in your project. You're a world-class virologist; any university or big pharma lab would take you. Your life isn't over."*

"This is my life's work. I don't care about universities or big pharma."

*"I have to go. Let's get together soon. I'll be in Berlin to open a new Muslim cultural center this June. I'll send you an invitation. I'd like you to come."*

Schumarr hung his head in despair. "Fine."

*"Thank you for your hard work."*

"Sure."

*"Goodbye, Barrett."*

Schumarr somberly walked the narrow and darkened passageways until he reached the lower decks where his research facility was located. He searched his thoughts for how he could save his work but nothing came.

He looked at his watch. There was thirty-seven minutes to go before the choppers arrived and ferried them all away. He hated the thought of abandoning years of work, but with Clayton overseeing the shutdown, he'd never be able to get one scrap of paper off the ship without him knowing about it.

"Dr. Schumarr, Dr. Schumarr!" Franz yelled from the other end of the passageway.

Schumarr looked up. He could see the distress on Franz's face.

"What's wrong?" Schumarr asked.

"It's Clayton. He's in your office…and he's destroying everything," Franz replied, out of breath.

Schumarr's eyes widened in shock. He sprinted past Franz and into the laboratory. His office lay in the far corner and there he saw Clayton and two other men ripping apart his logs and shredding the contents.

"No!" Schumarr barked, racing towards them.

"Stop him," Clayton ordered.

The two men who were helping Clayton grabbed Schumarr.

"Stop it!" Schumarr blared.

"I gave you the opportunity and I see you haven't done one thing," Clayton said, stuffing a stack of papers into a shredder.

"What does it matter? You're blowing up the ship!" he yelled.

Clayton grabbed another tall stack and began feeding the shredder. "I'm not taking any chances."

Schumarr tried to resist the grips of the men. "You're hurting me."

Clayton leaned close to Schumarr and barked, "Bring me everything of value. I need to destroy it myself."

A howl came from down the hall.

Clayton looked past Schumarr. "What was that?"

"That's Project Titan," Schumarr replied.

A devilish grin spread across Clayton's face. "I'd like to meet him." He stepped over stacks of binders and exited the room. "Where is he?"

"Let go of me. I'll show you," Schumarr said still struggling.

Clayton looked at his men and nodded. "Let him go."

Schumarr brushed himself off and straightened his wrinkled clothes. He reached into his pocket and removed a ring of keys. "Follow me."

Clayton and the others did just that.

Schumarr took them through a short maze, which ended in front of a large door. He peered through the small window in the door and saw three eighteen pacing; the triple restraints dangled from his wrists. In the far corner of the room, Schumarr took note of the observation window. Suddenly, an idea popped in his head. "He's in there, but we need to go to the observation room, this way." Schumarr took them around the corner and led them into a small darkened room. A single table with two chairs faced a large window.

"Here you'll get a better view of him," Schumarr said, pointing into the room.

Clayton and the two men walked in.

Three eighteen stopped pacing and looked around.

Schumarr turned on the light in the observation room.

Three eighteen snapped his head in the direction of the window. He sprinted towards it and launched himself forcefully but bounced off and fell to the floor.

Clayton and the others flinched but Schumarr didn't. "Bullet-resistant reinforced glass, level five like in armored vehicles."

Clayton replied with a simple grin. "You're prepared, I see."

"Yes," Schumarr said, taking a few steps back towards the entry door.

Three eighteen picked himself up, walked to the window and stared at everyone. Blood streamed down his face from a gash where his head had impacted the glass. His fully dilated eyes examined each of them on the other side.

"What's he doing?" Clayton asked.

"I'm not sure, as I haven't had ample time to study him, but if I were to guess, he's *studying* us."

"Fascinating," Clayton said.

"Fascinating, indeed," Schumarr said.

Three eighteen looked to his right and saw a door next to the window, which opened into the observation room. He stepped over and tried the handle but found it locked. He returned to staring at them.

"Does he always drool like that?" Clayton asked.

"I think so. Again, I haven't had time to examine him. He's unique," Schumarr said proudly.

"And what was it that made him this way?" Clayton asked, his eyes glued to the staring test subject.

"A parasite, a simple single-cell parasite."

Clayton craned his head towards Schumarr and said, "Parasite?"

"Yes, a common one too."

"What do you mean? Explain?"

Schumarr looked at his watch and saw the time. The helicopters would be arriving in twenty-three minutes. He needed to act and fast.

"Two years ago, I read a research white paper on a

common parasite called *Toxoplasma gondii*. It's been known for a while that it has the ability to control rats. What I found intriguing from this research was they believe it can affect humans too."

"How so?"

"By creating rage. They discovered that half of the people who display unprovoked anger issues are infected with this parasite. I found this fascinating. I began to think that if it could be sequenced properly, we could use this parasite to our advantage by creating a type of super soldier. With that in mind, I endeavored on doing just that. I took the parasite and enhanced its effects on the human hosts. Three eighteen is the first one to survive to this phase of testing."

"You're telling me this guy has a parasite in his brain?"

"Yes, one I've enhanced synthetically, a *Toxoplasma* on steroids, you could say."

"But…exactly how were you planning on weaponizing this?" Clayton asked. His face showed the confusion that was going through his mind. "You told us you were working on a virus, some sort of bioweapon but you were just making Frankenstein-type shit here."

"I'm working on Sleeper, but this can be weaponized. I'm just not there yet in my research. I need more time, but we could create a super soldier who is stronger, faster and wants nothing but to kill, imagine that."

"What's wrong with him? He just stands there staring," Clayton asked, facing the window again.

"I can only guess but the parasite seems to want to spread by attacking uninfected. It attacked and killed my assistant Charles but before Charles died, it appeared he was trying to infect him."

"Infect? What have you made here?" Clayton asked.

"Like I said, I need more time," Schumarr said.

"How dare you create this…whatever this is. When were you planning on telling me?" Clayton asked.

Schumarr didn't answer. He stepped out the door, slammed it shut and locked it.

"Dr. Schumarr, what are you doing?" Franz asked standing in the hallway.

"Ensuring our work continues," he replied to Franz.

Clayton ran to the closed door and began slamming his fists against it. "Open the door!"

"Sorry, but my work is too important," Schumarr said and slapped a large red button on the wall.

Inside the room, Clayton heard an audible click coming from the door that connected their room and the holding cell. He looked at the door then the window.

Three eighteen cocked his head at an angle and gazed upon the door. He reached for the handle, turned it and this time it opened.

"Schumarr, let us out of here!" Clayton yelled.

Three eighteen threw the door open, stepped into the open doorway and stared at Clayton and the two men.

"Kill him, kill him now!" Clayton ordered the two men.

The men stood frozen in fear.

"Kill him, damn you!" Clayton screamed.

Schumarr didn't wait to watch. He had little time to get what he needed and rushed off.

Three eighteen sprang on the first man and ripped his throat out then leapt onto the next.

Clayton frantically kept trying the handle of the locked door in a fruitless effort to open it. "Schumarr, open the door, please. I'll let you take your work, but please open the door!"

Schumarr raced to his office and grabbed a stack of his personal diaries and all the logs which represented years of work. He turned to Franz and ordered, "In the lab, get all the discs, hurry."

Screams came from the observation room.

Schumarr paused. It gave him pleasure when he imagined three eighteen ripping Clayton apart.

A loud crash came from down the hall.

Schumarr grabbed what he needed and ran out of his office. Movement down the long passageway caught his eye. He turned to see three eighteen's arm dangling out the small window in the door. *What have I created?* he asked himself a bit freaked out.

Franz came around the corner. "I have the discs."

"Let's hurry, come on," Schumarr said.

The two men sprinted until they reached a hatch that led to the flight deck.

Franz cranked the lever and pushed the heavy hatch open.

Daylight washed over them.

The first of two helicopters had landed and the crew were boarding.

"Our timing couldn't be better," Schumarr said with a smile.

The two made their way but were stopped by Steffen, the captain of the ship. "Where's Clayton?"

"Oh, he's down below. He'll catch the second helicopter," Schumarr replied. Beads of sweat poured down his face.

Steffen raised a single brow. "Really?"

Schumarr could see the doubt in Steffen's face. "Can we get on board now?"

"No, I was given specific instructions not to allow you on one of those birds unless Clayton was present. He's your escort off this thing."

"That's ridiculous," Schumarr rebuffed.

"No, what's ridiculous is you were working on a fucking uncontrollable monster that could have killed us all and you didn't seem to think you should tell me, the captain," Steffen reprimanded.

"I don't care what they told you, it's all a lie," Schumarr railed.

"Doesn't matter what you say, I listen to whoever pays me and that's not you. Now go over there and wait until Clayton comes up," Steffen ordered as he pointed to a crate fifteen feet away.

Schumarr clenched his teeth in frustration. He was so close to getting away but Clayton had covered all his bases.

"What now?" Franz asked.

The first helicopter lifted off; within minutes the second

landed. The remaining crew boarded and were now waiting for Clayton and his two men to appear but, of course, they weren't coming.

Steffen walked over to Schumarr and asked, "Where is he?"

"I don't know what you're talking about. Last I saw him was in my lab. He was destroying stuff."

"Stuff like that?" Steffen asked, pointing at the logs Schumarr was cradling like a small infant.

"No, these are my person diaries," Schumarr replied.

"Let me see," Steffen ordered, his hand stretched out.

"These are personal diaries," Schumarr barked.

"We don't have time for your bullshit. The first charge is set to go off in ten minutes and we were supposed to be airborne five minutes ago. Now tell me where Clayton is."

A figure stepped out a hatch and onto the deck.

Steffen turned but the sun was in his eyes. "Clayton is that you? Where the hell have you been?"

Schumarr nudged Franz, leaned in close and said, "Run."

And run he did. Franz sprinted for the helicopter with Schumarr just behind him.

"Hold on, where are you two going?" Steffen asked.

Schumarr didn't look back. He knew what was coming. When he heard Steffen wail in pain he ran harder.

The two reached the helicopter. Schumarr climbed on, but as Franz was, he dropped the dozens of floppy discs. "Shit!"

Frantically he began picking them up.

Schumarr looked and saw three eighteen sprinting towards the chopper. He yelled, "Lift off, lift off now!"

"Your friend?" the pilot hollered over the noise of the rotating blades.

"Go!" Schumarr snapped.

The chopper lifted, but Franz didn't notice, as he was focused on gathering the dozens of discs. When the chopper was a foot up and climbing, Franz looked up. "No, wait!"

"Leave him, go!" Schumarr wailed.

Franz reached, but Schumarr offered the sole of his shoe and kicked him. Franz fell back onto the deck. He turned to get up, but three eighteen was on him before he could react.

"Hurry, go, go!" Schumarr yelled.

The pilot did exactly that. He accelerated the chopper's ascent and in seconds was several hundred feet above the aft of the ship and climbing.

Schumarr looked down as three eighteen ripped Franz's body apart.

The man in the copilot chair tapped Schumarr on the shoulder and handed him a headset.

Schumarr put on the headset and was greeted by the pilot. "What was that thing on the deck?"

"It was beautiful," Schumarr replied.

A voice with a thick Middle Eastern accent then asked, "Are you Dr. Schumarr?"

Schumarr looked at the several faces on the chopper.

They were all familiar; he had known them for years and none had accents like this. Confused he asked, "Who's this?"

"My name is Aashiq. I'm a friend of Yasser," the voice said.

Schumarr kept looking at the faces in the back with him but no one was talking. He turned to the cockpit and stared.

The man in the copilot's seat turned and removed his sunglasses. "Hi, Dr. Schumarr, I'm Aashiq."

"Yasser didn't say anyone was coming."

In a slow but steady voice, Aashiq asked, "What did we just witness on the deck of the ship?"

"That was Project Titan," Schumarr replied.

"And what are you carrying with you?" Aashiq asked.

"Oh, um, these are my private diaries," Schumarr lied.

"Good Doctor, you were given specific instructions not to take anything off that ship."

"But these are my private and personal journals, nothing more," Schumarr pressed.

"And what happened to Mr. Clayton?"

"I think we can assume that subject three eighteen killed him," Schumarr said.

Distant explosions distracted Schumarr. He craned his head back to see the ship now engulfed in several large orange fireballs. When he faced Aashiq he was greeted with the muzzle of a semi-automatic pistol.

"Give me the journals," Aashiq ordered calmly.

"But they're—"

Aashiq leveled the muzzle at Schumarr's face and repeated, "Give me the journals."

Schumarr gulped. He thought quickly about what he could do, but now he had zero options save throwing himself and his journals out the open doorway of the helicopter with hopes he'd survive the fifteen-hundred-foot fall.

"Now," Aashiq pressed.

Schumarr couldn't hesitate anymore. He loosened his arms and handed over the logbooks.

Aashiq took them. He holstered the pistol and opened the first book on the stack. He read for a minute then began to flip through quickly.

"Project Sleeper is in book three," Schumarr said.

"I don't care about that. Where can I find everything on Titan?" Aashiq asked his attention still on the books.

"Titan?"

Aashiq looked back at Schumarr and asked, "Where's all the information on Titan?"

"If you wanted it, I could have just given the real thing to you," Schumarr said.

"You have it on you?"

"Um, no, I didn't get a chance to get a live sample but everything you need to know to replicate it is in book seven," Schumarr answered.

Aashiq put book seven on top and opened it, he flipped until he found a tab that read *TITAN*. "Of course. This is good, really good." Aashiq excitedly read, his finger tracing the words.

Schumarr relaxed into his seat. The fear he had that

his life was on the line melted away.

Aashiq read for ten minutes, closed the book, faced Schumarr and asked, "This is everything?"

"Everything...So Yasser *is* interested in Project Titan and not Sleeper?"

Aashiq held up book seven and asked again, "This is everything one needs to replicate the Titan parasite? How does it work? What's the R naught? Incubation?" Aashiq asked, rattling off questions.

"You seem to know a lot about this sort of stuff," Schumarr said.

"PhD in microbiology from Oxford."

"Impressive," Schumarr said with a half grin.

"Yasser speaks highly of you. I can see why, you're brilliant," Aashiq said.

"So you and I will be working on this?" Schumarr asked.

The helicopter turned left.

Schumarr looked through the cockpit window and could see the shoreline coming into view.

Aashiq tapped the pilot's arm and said, "Put us down on the far west side of the bay. There's a landing zone over there."

The pilot nodded.

"Where are we going?" Schumarr asked.

Aashiq turned back around and asked, "What I asked before, it's all in here? Incubation time, everything?"

"Yes, you'll see I'm thorough and detailed."

"And it does exactly as you say it does in here?"

"If you mean does it work to change a host, yes;

however, I don't know if it can spread from host to host and the incubation time is long. If I were to continue working on it, I'd dedicate time and resources to enhancing or accelerating the parasite's maturation."

"How did you create such a beautiful thing?" Aashiq gushed.

"Like I told Clayton, I follow where the science takes me." Schumarr glowed.

Aashiq couldn't believe his good luck.

"I still think some additional testing is needed to see how it mutates. And I need to see about creating a vaccine," Schumarr replied.

"But it's all here, it just needs to be perfected?" Aashiq asked still in shock at this discovery.

"It's all there. And you saw it with your own eyes. That was a man infected with the Titan parasite. It's real, it works."

Aashiq tenderly touched the cover of the logbook.

"Why didn't Yasser tell me earlier he was interested in Titan?" Schumarr asked.

"He's not, but when he told me about it, I was beyond thrilled. What's in here will ensure our caliphate rules the world and stamps out the infidel. This is it, this will bring about the end of days."

"I'm confused," Schumarr said.

"You're a brilliant scientist, Dr. Schumarr. Do you wish to continue your work?"

Not believing his luck, Schumarr smiled and said, "Nothing would give me more pleasure."

"Good."

"But on one condition," Schumarr pressed.

"And that is?" Aashiq asked.

"That I be allowed to take Titan to its fullest potential."

"Good Doctor, you'll be given every resource. We want nothing more than Titan to be as powerful as it can be," Aashiq replied.

"Excellent. When do we begin?"

"As soon as we land," Aashiq said and held his hand out to Schumarr. "It will be an honor to work alongside you on this most holy of endeavors."

Schumarr firmly grasped Aashiq's hand and shook it. "The honor is mine."

Aashiq turned towards the front. He cradled book seven against his chest, closed his eyes and said, "Praise be Allah."

Get **DAY OF RECKONING** exclusively on Amazon.

## ABOUT THE AUTHOR

G. Michael Hopf is the best-selling author of THE NEW WORLD series and other apocalyptic novels. He spent two decades living a life of adventure before he settled down and became a novelist full time. He is a combat veteran of the Marine Corps and a former executive protection agent. He lives with his family in San Diego, CA

Please feel free to contact him at geoff@gmichaelhopf.com with any questions or comments.

www.gmichaelhopf.com

www.facebook.com/gmichaelhopf

Books by G. MICHAEL HOPF

## THE NEW WORLD SERIES

THE END
THE LONG ROAD
SANCTUARY
THE LINE OF DEPARTURE
BLOOD, SWEAT & TEARS
THE RAZOR'S EDGE
THOSE WHO REMAIN

## NEW WORLD SERIES SPIN OFFS

NEMESIS: INCEPTION
EXIT

## ADDITIONAL BOOKS

HOPE (CO-AUTHORED W/ A. AMERICAN)
DAY OF RECKONING
MOTHER (EXTINCTION CYCLE SERIES)
DETACHMENT (PERSEID COLLAPSE SERIES)
DRIVER 8: A POST-APOCALYPTIC NOVEL

Made in the USA
Lexington, KY
18 April 2019